THE SCIENCE OF FRIENDSHIP

Also by Tanita S. Davis

Figure It Out, Henri Weldon
Partly Cloudy
Serena Says

Tanita S. Davis

THE SCIENCE OF FRIENDSHIP

HARPER

An Imprint of HarperCollins*Publishers*

Library of Congress Control Number: 2023944485
ISBN 978-0-06-328474-6

24 25 26 27 28 LBC 5 4 3 2 1
First Edition

To the Spite Sisters in my junior high class, who might not have known that, even if most of a story has been written, a revision is always an option.

1

What Happened Before

At 11:43 on May 27, Rylee Swanson thought Jackson McDonald was the *worst*.

At 11:55 on May 27, Rylee Swanson found out she was *totally* mistaken.

"Jackson! You're such a jerk!" Rylee yelled, slamming the sliding glass door behind her. On a beautiful, breezy morning in May, she'd been dangling her feet in the pool at her friend Nevaeh Green's house, minding her own business, when Jackson did a cannonball into the pool right next to her. One big splash, and Rylee's classy topknot and sideswept bangs were *wrecked*.

While Jackson laughed and high-fived the boys around him, Rylee did a fast-walk into the safety of the house, but it was too late. There was nothing to save of her cute updo. It wasn't even up anymore, but a falling-down mess of sad, saturated kinks.

"Snotheaded *jerk*," Rylee muttered. Grumpily, she located her duffel among the messy piles of her classmates' bags on Nevaeh's floor and tossed it on the end of the bed. She touched her hair again and sighed. She'd spent *so* much time making it look cute! And for nothing!

"Ignorant, bigheaded clown," Rylee fumed, giving up on her hair and struggling to get out of her totally drenched suit. At least the whole class hadn't been there to witness her humiliation. Not everyone had been invited to the party, and the few girls Rylee knew best had gone off somewhere—probably together— which was why Rylee had been sitting alone by the pool in the first place.

It could have been worse. Though Rylee knew many of her classmates at Segrest, where she attended, she hadn't known the people around the pool very well. Now that she'd been splashed, she was glad she'd been sitting alone. If the girls she hung out with had been there, they would have noticed Jackson's cannonball, and they might have laughed at her. As it was, the boys would probably lure Jackson into playing Marco

Polo or have another water fight in a few minutes, and they'd forget all about her.

And, if Rylee was already forcing herself to look on the bright side, she should be grateful that she was alone in Nevaeh's pretty, ruffled bedroom with the built-in dressers, matching princess bed, and framed posters on the wall. Nevaeh, who had transferred to their school midyear in sixth, could be super nice sometimes, but today wasn't one of those days. Rylee had already seen her exchanging meaningful glances with Aaliyah when she'd arrived, and Rylee had heard Cherise whispering to Rosario to "look at her bathing suit!" Rylee wasn't sure what was up with everyone that day, but she was just as glad not to have an audience now.

The one-piece with the bike shorts and skirt that the saleslady had called a "swim romper" was mostly baggy, and modest, and all the other things Mom liked, but when wet it somehow still managed to stick to her like a ruffled black suction cup. Getting it off was *not* graceful. Getting it off a chilly body—it really wasn't warm enough for a pool party yet—was even worse. After a lot of wriggling and puffing, Rylee rolled the soggy suit into her towel with a defeated sigh. Mom and Rylee had only found an "okay" suit in her size, but her hair had looked *amazing*. Now, thanks to *stupid* Jackson, she'd have to spend the next ten minutes in the bathroom blotting the water with a microfiber towel, uncoiling the kinks, and pulling her hair back as tightly as she could into a plain old, everyday ponytail until she could get home to rinse the chlorine out.

Rylee grabbed the zipper of her duffel bag and yanked—and stopped. She sucked in a breath, alarm raising the tiny hairs on her arms.

There was her lotion, her deodorant, and her wide-toothed comb. There was her Coconut Mist body spray, which smelled so good it always made her hungry. There was the little wallet that held five dollars in quarters for the bus, her hair bands, and her super shiny Shimmer Smile lip gloss. The rest of the bag held . . . nothing. No bra, no underwear, no shorts, no long red T-shirt. Nothing.

Baffled, Rylee checked the side of the bag, assuring herself that the familiar pink-and-white stripes and anchor decal were actually hers. She frantically riffled through the piles of towels and jeans on the floor. Maybe someone had opened her bag, thinking it was theirs, and her clothes had fallen out—? No? Eyes wide and agitated, Rylee looked in the bag again.

Nothing.

Rylee walked in a tight circle, gaze darting from the bag to the door and back. She clutched her clammy swimsuit. She just couldn't *stand* there. What if someone came *in* while she wasn't wearing clothes?

Rylee wrapped her arms around herself, aware of just how little of her own body she could cover. Should she put the cold, wet suit back on and find someone who would help her search? Rylee looked at the door. She could stand behind it and lean out, and maybe whisper-shout for Rosario, or Aaliyah, to come and help her? Nevaeh was the hostess, so she was probably busy helping her mom, and Cherise—well, she was sometimes a little salty when you asked her for favors. Could she even get back into the suit when it was wet? Mrs. Green was in the kitchen, but . . . no. This was embarrassing enough.

Rylee looked at her bag again, and then at the haphazard piles of other bags on the bed. All of them were zipped. This was *so* weird, but . . . it couldn't be what she was thinking. Nobody would *do* something like this on purpose. . . .

Rylee dropped to her knees and peered under the bed. From behind her, there came a muffled noise.

Creak.

A chorus of giggles.

No. Oh *no.*

Rylee's wet skin pebbled with goose bumps as she wrapped her arms around herself, trying to hold herself together. Her chest burned as she fought for air, coming stiffly to her feet in the middle of the room. Someone was watching. Someone was there, while she crawled around without clothes. And whomever it was, they were *laughing* at her.

Being laughed at while also being wet, and cold, and worried?

This, Rylee was certain, was the absolute *worst.*

The *Segrest Sentinel* Reports

SEGREST STANDPOINTS: Five Reasons You Should Join the *Segrest Sentinel*

by Nathan Tan, news editor

***

The ~~views and~~ *opinions expressed in the Segrest Sentinel are those of the students and do not necessarily reflect the official policies* ~~or positions~~ *of Segrest School. Survey responses may have been edited for length or clarity.*

***

The *Segrest Sentinel* is published once a month online and in print. I~~n~~ the student handbook~~, it says~~ states that the school paper "gives students the opportunity to act as reporters and focus on creative thinking, teamwork, interviews, writing, editing, artwork, design, and layout."

More important than those reasons for joining the school paper, the *Segrest Sentinel* is the voice of the student body.

Every student should take advantage of the freedom to ask questions, make statements, and express themselves about the things that matter to them in a space where it's safe for a person to speak and where others will listen with respect. ¶While social media provides a lot of places for people to say what they want, it's a noisy place where you risk not being heard.

The *Sentinel* gives writers an audience of others who care about what they're saying, and because it's our school paper, it belongs to ^of all us. Every student can participate and get involved instead of just being spectators while those who type the fastest or have more followers get to take center stage.

Researching a story, working with advertisers, taking pictures, or drawing comics will give staff new skills and opportunities to talk with people they wouldn't have otherwise met. *Sentinel* staff learn things about the segrest community, the school administration, and themselves that can then benefit the Segrest student body as a whole.

Five reasons you should join the school paper are:

1. The *Sentinel* is a place for every student's voice.
2. The press is mightier than social media.
3. You'll improve your writing and other skills.
4. You'll learn to work with all kinds of people and meet new people.
5. It's actually fun.

Segrest School, make your voices heard!

2

Survival Strategy

"Now, that's what I'm talking about!" Rylee's grandmother Geema applauded as Rylee finally came out of her bedroom and into the kitchen. "There she is. Twirl, girl!"

"Gee*maaa*," Rylee groaned, covering her face with her hands. Her grandmother's over-the-top energy on the first day of school was something Rylee should have been prepared for but never was. Geema was probably more excited about Rylee's first-day outfit than all the *Teen Vogue* editors were about the first day of fashion week.

"Don't make me get up and help you now." The tall woman in the velour navy tracksuit settled back into her seat at the table and gestured regally. "You look beautiful. Go back and give me a runway strut."

With reluctant steps, Rylee turned around to reenter the kitchen, turning first one way and then the other, to let Geema see her outfit. As her grandmother's applause warmed her, Rylee's movements got bigger. She made exaggerated poses and blew kisses to imaginary paparazzi. As always happened when Rylee joined Geema's silliness, Geema went all out, humming upbeat music and drumming on the table next to her coffee cup while Rylee twirled and paraded.

"Go, Rylee! Go, Rylee!" Geema chanted.

Rylee snapped into another pose, pursing her lips and narrowing her eyes.

The world of make-believe fashion shattered abruptly as an amused voice said, "You know, I'm afraid to even ask what you two are supposed to be doing in here."

Rylee jumped, nearly tripping as she flailed. "Mom!" she squeaked.

"That's me," her mother said, a tiny smile tucking in the corners of her mouth. "You have everything you need for today? Or did you decide to drop out of eighth grade this year to strut the catwalk instead?"

"I'm coming. Geema just wanted to see my outfit," Rylee grumbled, grateful her brother, Axel, was already out front, awaiting his car pool. It was bad enough that Mom was there, in her serious work suit and a blouse in a color she called mauve but Rylee could only think of as purply brown.

"And that outfit looks *sharp*," Geema said, unbothered by Mom's amusement. "Eighth grade looks good on our girl." Geema reached out and smoothed Rylee's shirt a little as she turned her granddaughter to face her. "You're going to have a *great* day today; I can feel it."

Geema was right: Rylee *did* look good. Reflected in the glass doors by the second-floor drinking fountain, her cropped khaki pants, white platform sneakers, and oversize blue T-shirt were still on point and put together by the time she got to school. Mom had let her get dark blue hair extensions, and Rylee had braided them into two coils smoothly wound on the top of her head. Carrying her new navy backpack printed with orange poppies over one shoulder, Rylee looked fierce. Calm. Ready for her first day as an eighth grader at Segrest School.

So why did fear arc through her body like a zing of

12

electricity when she saw Nevaeh and Aaliyah in the hallway after the Wednesday Forum assembly?

Rylee immediately flung herself around the corner to hide, hardly able to breathe. She hadn't seen any of her so-called friends since the pool party in May. It had been three months. . . . Had they seen her? Were they going to— Rylee closed her eyes, breathing in noisily to cover the remembered sound of the giggles that had erupted when she'd crouched to look under the bed, that head-shaking, pitying side-eye Nevaeh had given her at the end. . . .

But nothing happened. No one called her name as she stood frozen and tense in the hallway of the eighth-grade wing. Rylee exhaled and straightened shakily, glancing around to see if anyone had noticed her. Even though she had a water bottle in her backpack, Rylee leaned her wrist against the bar for the drinking fountain, filling her mouth with liquid so cold her teeth ached.

Right. Okay. She needed to get moving.

At least it hadn't been Rosario and Cherise standing around in the hallway, too. The Spite Sisters, as Rylee had started thinking of them, hadn't texted or called, and Rylee had found herself alone in her room through the long summer days. She had haunted their socials, praying no one had posted any pictures of her, watching to find any mentions. She'd been treated instead to a painful parade of pool parties, amusement parks, sleepovers, and movies in the park as her former friends had enjoyed their vacation. Mom had tried asking, the week after the pool party, if something was wrong, but so far, Rylee couldn't even talk about it. After so many weeks, the whole swim party thing was over anyway, right? Those girls were trash, the friendship was *over*, and Rylee didn't care if they all fell in a hole; she was so done. So, why weren't these *feelings* going away, too?

For something to do, Rylee squatted down and opened her backpack, double-checking that her phone was on silent.

Normally, she would have known what she was walking into on the first day. She would have uploaded a snap of the class schedule she'd gotten in the mail and seen everyone's in return. She would have met the girls at the rose circle on the lawn at the front of the administration building, and they would have all checked out each other's outfits and done last-minute snack swaps so they could survive until lunch. She would have had people to be with during the one and only Wednesday Forum without assigned seating, and they could have shared quiet giggles while mimicking Principal Loughran-Smith's catchphrases together. This year, Rylee hadn't shared anything with anyone . . . and nobody had asked.

Instead, the first day of school that year felt like a giant chasm the size of the Grand Canyon had opened up between Rylee and everyone else, a humongous hole in the world that she would never, ever be able to build a bridge long enough to get over. She felt like she was always going to be the only one at Segrest who had no friends, and no one to talk to, and it was *horrible*.

Rylee blew out a hard breath and straightened, zipping her bag.

She was fine. No one had ever died of nervousness.

Rylee was still alive after the first day of *sixth* grade, and *that* had been a day too terrifying for words at the time.

Even though she was nervous, Rylee would get through the first—extra short—day of eighth grade without dying. The first step: fifteen minutes of homeroom.

Squaring her shoulders, Rylee turned resolutely toward room 6, where today she would have Ms. Johnston three times: for homeroom, journalism for elective period, and advisory at the end of the day. At least she was kind of familiar—Ms. Johnston had given a talk on truth and facts in the news for English Language Arts when they'd done newspaper assignments in sixth grade. Rylee barely remembered her, but she'd had a nice smile.

Rylee was counting on that smile as she nervously threaded her way through the denizens of the hallway, ducking and eeling her way through the mass of moving bodies. Students were chatting. Looking at phones. Waving. Laughing. So many big grins, slapped shoulders, hugs. The goofy nudge-and-shove of in-joke giggles. All around, people connecting with their people.

Their *people*. Rylee shoved down the memory of muffled giggles again. She'd thought she had people, once. She'd thought the friends she'd made at the beginning of junior high would last at least until high school. But here she was, starting all over again—not sure where to sit, or who to talk to, or what to talk about.

Whatever. Teachers always said you weren't at school to make friends anyway. Rylee swallowed hard again and lifted her chin, hoping the expression she had on her face looked determined and not like she was forcing herself not to run to the bathroom and hide.

"Good morning. Come on in." Ms. Johnston urged Rylee in from the doorway, the smile Rylee remembered shining from her face like a break in the clouds. "Grab a seat anywhere you find one."

Rylee dodged the clump of boys aiming for seats in the back row and headed toward the bank of windows on the left side of the room. She looked for an empty seat in the front but hesitated when she encountered a massive gray backpack sitting open in the middle of the aisle, leaking books, pens, and notebooks in an untidy jumble that blocked her path.

"Um . . . hello?" Rylee said.

"Sorry, just a sec," said a voice from the floor.

Rylee raised her eyebrows as a girl with pretty brown skin and short dark curls scrambled around on hands and knees to return a handful of permanent markers to a pocket in her bag. Rylee counted six colorful notebooks, a laptop, and a pair of socks before the bag was closed and tugged out of the aisle. Did she *live* in that thing?

"So . . . were socks on the school supply list, and I missed it?" Rylee blurted before she could stop herself.

"Hah," the girl said, sounding distinctly unamused

as she crammed a few more stray pens into a side pocket. "Sorry," she repeated, finally shoving the giant backpack behind her desk. "My parents are separated. . . . I used this bag to pack for a weekend at my dad's, and it's still not quite . . . unpacked." The girl gave Rylee a quick glance, straightening the beaded headband decorating her short hair.

"Oh. Yeah. Hate that," Rylee said, even though she had never visited her father, ever. Mom had moved them in with Geema and Daddy Warren before Axel had been big enough to walk, and Rylee barely recalled his face.

"I'm DeNia Alonso. I remember you—Rylee, right? You made mood-ring slime for fifth-grade science fair."

"Um . . . yeeeah?" Rylee said doubtfully. She'd thought the girl was new—she couldn't remember seeing her around. And who kept track of science fair projects? "And you made—?"

"I made the naked eggs." The girl grinned and fiddled with the stack of black rubber bracelets around her wrist. "I soaked raw eggs in different acids to see how long it took the shells to dissolve."

Rylee straightened, surprised when a vague scent-memory of a fifth-grade science project surfaced in her mind. "Oh, yeah! Those were kind of gross. I

18

remember being completely shocked that orange juice makes brown eggs white."

DeNia grinned. "Yep. It was the most basic experiment *ever*, but it was fun." She gestured at the desk across from her. "There's no one sitting there," she invited.

Rylee hesitated. Maybe DeNia would turn out to be awful—Rylee didn't trust her friend judgment anymore—but she seemed pretty harmless with her talk about science fairs, *and* she for sure hadn't been at Nevaeh's party. Rylee shrugged and dropped into the seat.

"Thanks," she said. "I'm sure your science projects were no more basic than mine. It's not like slime was all that exciting. I'm pretty sure I got a participation ribbon for that in fifth."

"Because everyone made slime," DeNia nodded knowledgeably. "And then, the next year you did a collaborative project, and unless they're amazing, those don't usually get anything but participation ribbons, either."

Rylee blinked. She barely remembered sixth-grade science at all. "You . . . How do you know what I did for science fair projects?"

"I know what everyone did," DeNia said with a

shrug, fiddling with her bracelets again. "I've kept a file on all the science fair projects for my grade since fifth."

"Oh, so that's . . . interesting," Rylee said politely. What she really wanted to ask was, *Are you serious with this right now?* but that seemed rude. "Sounds like a lot of work."

"It's not," DeNia said. "The state keeps track of projects for a lot of schools, and you can look it up online. It's good to know who the competition is before you get out there. I mean—if you're serious like I am."

"Uh-*huh*." Okay, that was just *too* random. Rylee hoped her face didn't show how she felt. She was embarrassed for DeNia. Science was fine, of course— people did things with science like save sick people from dying or whatever, but nobody Rylee knew was so obviously *into* things like that—not until they were in high school, at least.

Rylee liked a lot of stuff—riding her bike on the canal trail, trying to fill in crosswords with Daddy Warren, and cooking with Geema, for instance—but none of that really added up to anything she'd say she was *serious* about. It was just . . . stuff she did.

Rylee made a show of glancing around the room and smiling vaguely at the other students as DeNia dropped to the floor to dig in her giant backpack again. As the stack of notebooks—and was that a cereal bowl!?—rose again, Rylee eyed the mess with distaste. This chaos was a *lot*. She should have known better than to sit with the first person who talked to her. Rylee imagined her old friends watching DeNia with her. Nevaeh would come up with one of her nicknames and call her Backpack Betty or something, and Aaliyah would widen her eyes and say that DeNia was "a little intense."

Ugh. She should move. Rylee looked around for another open desk, but Ms. Johnston was closing the classroom door.

"Find a seat, everyone," she called, as familiar upbeat music came from the flat-screen monitor mounted on the wall. Rylee sighed and turned her attention to the Segrest School Morning Show, pulling out her school-issued laptop to answer the poll question on the screen that would count her present for class. The first-day question was completely silly, of course. *If Segrest School were a breed of dog, what breed would it be?* Rylee hesitated between German shepherd and the hyper-looking collie before choosing one. With the brief broadcast full of school-wide announcements and the welcome blather finished, Ms. Johnston stood once again at her podium, smiling widely.

"I hope you're all prepared to get the most out of your first day at Segrest. You'll notice there are a lot of new faces this year, and you'll see many of this same group at sixth period for advisory. We're going to really get to know one another this year . . ."

Rylee stifled a yawn and looked across the aisle and over her shoulder. It seemed like every year, every single teacher had to give their whole five-minute welcome talk, and the whole room was already bored. DeNia was once again bent over, rummaging in her . . . well, it was *luggage*—there was really no other word for a backpack that big. Rylee rolled her eyes. It was like she was one of those hamsters that stuffed things in their mouths until they got all bulky. Rylee could totally see her like that, some kind of Pack Rat Patty.

Rylee smirked and turned away, her glance tangling with another girl with familiar arched eyebrows, and waist-length braids. She was also watching DeNia, eyes exaggeratedly wide with distaste.

Rylee sucked in a breath, scenes from the pool party flooding her mind.

Her brain felt like cotton stuffing was wrapped around it, but slowly, she was beginning to understand. Her missing friends, the sneak attack from Jackson, who usually didn't act like he knew Rylee was alive, the suspiciously empty bedroom and the quiet house. This was a prank, a test, maybe. One of Neveah's little jokes she sometimes played.

Rylee clutched her arms against the front of her body and swallowed hard, peering into the empty room's corners. "Um, hello?" she asked, her voice small in the suddenly huge space.

Silence.

"I need my clothes," Rylee said to the listening air, trying to sound fun but firm. They were only joking, and Rylee was totally a good sport. "Please?"

With an effort, Rylee relaxed her fingers, feeling the pain from the half-circle grooves her nails had left in her palms. How could she have missed seeing her? She hadn't been in the room full of people looking for seats—but, no. The coqueen of the Spite Sisters, Aaliyah Washington, liked to hold court in the hallway until the last second before the bell. She'd slipped into Rylee's homeroom like a dark shadow, right under Rylee's nose.

Wonderful.

The giant hole between Rylee and everyone else got two feet wider.

3

Headline News

Things didn't get better from there, unfortunately.

As Rylee walked down the hallway between classes, the feeling that she was on her own island grew. Conversations ebbed and flowed around her, excluding her. When she was in the bathroom checking her lip gloss and listening to the girls clustered around the mirrors talking about what they'd done over the summer, she'd felt like they were speaking a language she didn't know. Then she heard her name.

"Um, Rylee?"

"Yeah?" Rylee turned eagerly to the tall girl behind her—Meryl, who had been in her social studies class last year. Meryl nodded to the sink, holding up her hands.

"Could I—?"

"Oh—sorry. Sure, you can—go ahead. Sorry." Rylee's face flushed hot.

Standing around in the bathroom pretending she was part of a conversation was pathetic anyway. Rylee hurried to the next class and took the first empty desk she saw in the third row—far enough from the back row to avoid looking like a slacker, but not right in the front row with the teacher staring into her face.

Journalism was probably going to be an easy A, but all Rylee could think about was how she'd planned to be in Culinary Arts II and STEAM Robotics with her besties. She'd really been looking forward to making sourdough starters and swan-shaped cream puffs and coding movements for the robot dog, Rovr, built by the eighth graders last year.

But, after what happened, Rylee switched her electives to Journalism II and Chorus.

Nevaeh, Aaliyah, Rosario, and Cherise had taken the best of everything and ruined it.

"For those of you who are new," Ms. Johnston was saying, shrugging out of her lemon-yellow cardigan and quickly waking her laptop, "our journalism elective is where we use our natural curiosity to develop stories. Reporters are observers. They look at the world and find the answers that the public needs to know.

"Those of you who have previously worked on the *Sentinel*, please raise your hands," Ms. Johnston continued. "New folks, these students have experience you can use, and I know they'll be happy to share that with you."

Rylee took a quick glance around the room and did a double take as she spotted an excitedly waving arm. Seriously? DeNia, the science fair girl, was in journalism, too? Rylee almost laughed, a little relieved to see a familiar face—until she recognized someone else. Meeta Singh.

Rylee turned to face the front, swallowing in a suddenly tightening throat. Meeta had worn an adorable pink plaid tankini to Nevaeh's pool party. Rylee wondered uneasily if she was only imagining Meeta's loud laugh when Jackson's cannonball splashed her.

"So, the rule of three makes sure everyone has an opportunity to contribute, and everyone has equal opportunity to earn an A. As you can see"— Ms. Johnston shined a tiny laser pointer at the slide that appeared on the whiteboard—"every student is responsible for three pieces for the *Sentinel* per month. That might be an article or a student profile, a review or an interview, a creative piece, or something else. In order to keep our paper afloat, and to make points for your grade, you'll need to contribute. Each of you can submit *more* than three pieces, of course, but three pieces is the requirement and is worth ten percent of your grade.

"And don't forget we also need fact-checkers, copy editors, and proofreaders to make sure our reporting is the best it can be, fair and ethical." Ms. Johnston changed slides, and Rylee slumped at the long list of terms that appeared.

Snore. She couldn't believe Ms. Johnston was making them read a vocabulary list. This was supposed to be an elective, and electives were supposed to be fun. *In culinary class,* Rylee thought glumly, *we would have already put something in the oven by now.*

Maybe there was still time to switch out of this elective again and find something else to do. Would they let her take another semester of beginning Spanish?

"So, let's brainstorm a bit and see if we can pull together some news stories," Ms. Johnston finished. "If you get stuck, try pitching your idea as a title, or a headline."

Oh. Whoops, people were standing up, pushing desks together and moving into disorganized groups of two or three. Rylee had blanked out, but Ms. Johnston had said something about story ideas. . . . A quick glance around the room showed some people pairing up and opening their laptops. DeNia and Meeta had moved their desks apart, and Meeta was now sitting next to a red-haired boy and another tall girl. Rylee felt a spurt of alarm. Who was she supposed to work with? Did she *have* to work with a group?

The girls closest to Rylee had paired up, but one looked Rylee's way. Automatically, Rylee opened her laptop and clicked through to a blank screen in her computer. She typed, her keystrokes brisk and important: **Rylee Swanson, 5th Period.**

Everyone was tuned in to their groups, seeming to accept that she was working alone. For a moment, Rylee felt her shoulders slump with a mixture of relief and regret. The girls looking at her didn't *look* mean—it would have been easy to turn her desk and join them. But . . . they might not have been all that friendly. You couldn't tell by looking at people. And anyway, one of them might have been at the party, too.

Rylee chewed her lip, shooting a sidelong look at the two girls again. She sort of knew them. The Korean girl with the pencil shoved in her messy bun was Nicie Im, whose full name was Eunice, but after she'd given Mike Jones a bloody nose in fourth grade, nobody called her that to her face. Rylee remembered that Nicie and her friend, Dawn Something, had won the state spelling bee in the fifth grade. Rylee studied them. Was Nicie still competing? Were people who won those big spelling bees really good spellers in real life, or did they just memorize lists of words and use spell-check programs like everyone else? Did they like weird words and use them?

That might be a good pitch idea. Rylee typed, **Spelling Bee Champ: My Favorite Word.**

B*ooooo*ring. Was that all she could come up with?

Rylee's eyes strayed to the front of the room. Ms. Johnston was perched on the corner of her desk, reading something. The dark blue pants she wore reminded Rylee of the blue coveralls the janitor had been wearing that morning when Rylee had overheard him telling someone that he'd see if there was a hole up under the eaves. "If it's a bat, we're going to have to evacuate," he'd added over his shoulder, shaking the big flashlight he carried.

Rylee typed, **EVACUATE! What Pests Are in Our School Buildings?**

That was *much* better. Ms. Johnston had said their ideas needed to provoke a reaction from their readers.

Everyone would have a reaction to that headline.

The door opened a crack, and one of the ladies who worked in the school office slipped in from the hallway, meeting Ms. Johnston's smile with one of her own. With a brief comment, she handed a slip of paper to Ms. Johnston, who glanced at the sheet and murmured something back. They both laughed silently, the office lady putting a hand over her mouth and shaking her head. Then, the office lady waggled her fingers and stepped out as quietly as she'd arrived.

Rylee realized she was staring. It was just so *weird* to see teachers as . . . people. People who laughed with their coworkers or maybe were friends.

Friendships were so random. You never could predict who would hang out with whom. Like Geema and Ms. Grace—Geema preferred to wear either leopard-print everything, or rhinestones, while Ms. Grace was so formal and old-fashioned, she hardly ever wore pants, much less animal-print jeans. They were nothing alike, and they still hung out.

Rylee had the best group of weird friends in grade school—she wondered what had happened to them. She could pitch something about that— something about old friends and how elementary school friendships were great, not like the so-called friends you got in junior high. . . .

"Hey. So, Rylee," DeNia was suddenly crouching next to Rylee's desk, her expression full of eager friendliness. "Did you want to work together? Ms. Johnston said we could share a byline, and it'd be fun to work with you."

Rylee jolted, totally caught off guard. "Uh—hey, DeNia."

DeNia continued talking into Rylee's awkward silence. "Um . . . if you don't have an idea, some of us discussed doing teacher interviews—we have four new teachers this year. We could go in and do one together. Or, we can interview new students or something— does that sound good? What do you think?"

What Rylee thought was that interviewing anyone sounded boring, but she didn't say so. DeNia was trying to be nice, she reminded herself.

"Um—thanks, but I think this first round, I should, um, pitch my own stuff." Rylee's words sped up as her excuse took shape in her mind. "I mean, since you were on the *Sentinel* before, it's not really fair of me to glom on to one of your pieces. I have to learn to pitch by myself first, you know? But thanks."

DeNia looked confused. "If that's what you want to do, okay, but seriously, Ms. Johnston suggested we pair up and help the newbies, and sharing a byline is a good way to get started. I think she kind of *wants* you guys to lean on those of us who know what we're doing, but—"

"I know what I'm doing," Rylee sputtered. "I mean, yeah, I'm new, but I can write a paragraph."

DeNia shrugged. "Yeah, sure you can," she said easily. "But news writing is kind of harder than it looks. It's different from just regular writing." DeNia shrugged again and stepped back. "Anyway . . . let me know if you change your mind or need help or something."

If she needed *help*!? Rylee huffed an incredulous breath as she watched DeNia return to her seat in a cluster of desks at the back of the room. "'Those of us who know what we're doing,'" Rylee echoed, rolling her eyes. "Is she for real?"

Seriously, some people were just way too full of themselves.

4

Project

"That's thirty minutes, Axel!" Rylee yelled through her open doorway.

From his room across the hall, Rylee heard her brother, Alex—who'd renamed himself Axel when he'd discovered at six that letters switched around made fun, new words—give an acknowledging grunt. At least Rylee hoped that grunt meant he'd heard her. When he wasn't talking to his friends online, Axel didn't always pay that much attention.

Axel was *supposed* to do his homework before he got stuck on one of his computer games, but he never did. He always was "going to check just one thing" that turned into twenty things, into Mom getting home, and dinner being served, and Axel not having started . . . anything until an hour before he was supposed to go to bed. Mom and Axel had fussed so much about it last year that even Daddy Warren had noticed—which Mom said wasn't good for his blood pressure.

This year, Mom had asked Rylee to help out. She was supposed to "remind" Axel to get started. This was supposed to cut down on Mom and Axel fighting and Daddy Warren getting involved.

Rylee had had her doubts. First, there was nothing she could do to keep Daddy Warren out of anything if he decided to be involved. Second, reminders or no, Axel didn't sleep, work, eat, or do anything else unless he decided he wanted to—Daddy Warren's kind of stubborn ran in the family. So, Rylee talked it over with Axel and came up with a secret compromise: she'd time Axel for thirty minutes of video games as soon as he got home—just to check on all his campaigns and to make sure his little deals and tasks had been completed to his satisfaction—and *then* he would turn everything off to do his homework. In return for the reminder to stop playing, Axel owed Rylee one small favor a week, to be agreed on later.

It probably wasn't exactly "helping out," like Mom wanted, but so far, so good.

Right now, it was just after five o'clock, but already Rylee heard a jingle of keys.

"Axel, you'd better be working," Rylee hissed as she stood in her doorway. "Mom?"

"Yep, it's me," her mother called, quickly climbing the stairs barefoot, the straps of her work shoes looped over the fingers of one hand while her shoulder bag dangled from the other. She gave Rylee a big squeeze, then looked into Axel's room and pressed a kiss atop his head. "How's my boy?"

Axel mumbled something.

"You're almost done with that math?"

"No," Axel admitted, "but it's not that much. I got it."

"That's what we like to hear," Mom said, and leaned in to kiss him again.

"Mom!" Axel ducked, having reached his limit.

"Gotcha," Mom said, poking his unprotected sides.

Leaving Axel giggling like someone much younger than eleven, Rylee followed her mother to her bedroom at the end of the hall. She hovered in the doorway of the bright, airy space, admiring, as she always did, the faux-sheepskin rugs, sheer white drapes and white blinds, and fuzzy textured throw pillows on the white-quilted queen bed. Her mother's room looked like what Rylee imagined a perfect, soft snowbank felt like without the cold.

She shifted her glance to her mother. "So, you're home early."

"I worked through lunch. I wanted to get down to the Auto Mall and take a look around."

"We're getting a new car?" Rylee gasped, already excited.

"It'll be new to you," her mother's voice came from the closet where she was hanging up her work clothes. "I'm not up for new car payments, but your Geema threatened to start car shopping *for* me the last time Daddy changed the oil, so I'm just getting ahead of her."

Rylee grinned. Once Geema started shopping, it was hard to stop her. "Good luck."

"I'll need it." Her mother went into the bathroom to wash her face, and Rylee heard her voice rise over the running water. "So, how was school? Did all your friends like your fashion show outfit?"

Rylee stalled, unsure what to say. Mom didn't know how suddenly invisible she'd become to her former friends. "Uh . . . well, no one really commented," she offered, trying to be as honest as possible. "It's been kind of busy, you know? First week . . ."

"Hmm." Mom padded out of the bathroom in an oversize plaid shirt and soft leggings with her hair tucked under a satin-lined beanie. Though her clothes looked comfy and softer, Rylee felt a twist of dread as her mother hopped up on the bed and looked at Rylee with a penetrating gaze. "You still hanging out with Ms. Grace's granddaughter, Aaliyah?"

Rylee curled her toes against the hall carpet. "Not really."

"So that means you're not hanging out with Nevaeh or your other friends, either." Mom narrowed her eyes thoughtfully and patted the bed in invitation. "Come in and talk to me, Rylee. I've been wondering if something was going on. You stopped going to your Geema's church this past summer and started coming with me—and none of your friends attend my church. What's up?"

Nobody went into Mom's white-carpeted sanctuary without an invitation, but for once Rylee wished she hadn't been given one.

"Nothing's really going on?" She hated how her voice made the words a question. "I mean, at the pool party we kind of . . . they kind of . . ." Rylee's hands flailed, then fisted. "I guess they were just messing around, but it wasn't . . . nice."

"Oh. Tell me about it, Ry," her mother said, and reached for her.

Rylee panicked at the stinging in her eyes. Not *now!* she thought to her tears. "It's nothing," she said aloud, stepping away from her mother's arms and blinking rapidly. "We're—we just grew out of each other or whatever." Rylee flapped a hand unconvincingly. "You know how it goes. It's fine."

Mom let Rylee reclaim her distance, then held up a finger in a *wait* gesture. Scootching back on the bed, she reached into her nightstand drawer and pulled out a bag of black licorice drops.

"No, thank you," Rylee said, wrinkling her nose at the offer. Black licorice tasted like soap.

"Oh, I forgot, you don't eat the good stuff. Hang on, I've got you." Her mother pulled out a stack of magazines and a laptop, then dug deeper into the drawer before holding aloft a small bag of sour gummies. "Here. Have some of these nasty things."

Rylee smiled and sat on the end of the bed. Mom didn't like sour anything, so she knew these were in the drawer just for her. "Thanks, Mama."

Tucking a licorice drop into her cheek, Mom leaned back against the headboard and regarded Rylee again, an eyebrow raised. "So, you're on the outs with your girls. You sure you don't want to talk about it?"

Rylee bit an end off her sour worm and rolled it between her teeth. After the party, she'd lurked on her class message boards and social media, digging to see if there were any rumors or reasons she could find. She'd never found anything more than "if you know, you know" kinds of jokes, and comments she didn't understand. Getting splashed wasn't exactly big news at a pool party. And nobody who had been in Nevaeh's room had started a rumor about the girl who'd lost her clothes. At least not yet.

"Yeah . . . there's nothing really to talk about," Rylee said finally. "Aaliyah isn't . . . She and I don't really have all that much in common anyway."

Mom exhaled a long sigh, pulling her knees to her chest. "Mm-hmm. You know, something like this happened to me. In eighth grade, Lissa Shaw saw her boyfriend asking me something after school, and he wouldn't tell her what it was about, so . . . she told all the girls in our class that I was trying to steal him."

"Really?" Rylee blinked. "That's random."

Mom shrugged. "After that, none of the girls in our class with boyfriends talked to me for the whole semester, just because Lissa Shaw's boyfriend couldn't remember the English assignment. It was pretty bad."

Rylee frowned. "Wasn't Lissa Shaw the girl who nominated you for prom queen your senior year, though?"

"The very same," Mom snorted. "She always was kind of a bad friend. A frenemy."

"Why didn't her boyfriend just *tell* her? I can't believe all the girls wouldn't talk to you." Rylee rubbed her arms, feeling chilled at the idea. "Mom, what did you *do*? How did you get them to stop?"

"I didn't," Mom said, shifting the licorice to the other cheek. She shrugged. "I got used to being alone. I ate lunch by myself with a big, fat book, and finished half my homework before I got home."

Rylee sucked in a breath at the image of a lonely girl eating lunch at a table alone, as Rylee had done her first day of school. Mom had had nowhere to belong for weeks, stranded on her own side of the Grand Canyon of friend breakups, with no way across. "For the whole semester!? That's not fair!" she burst out. "You hadn't even *done* anything!"

Mom prodded Rylee's hip with a sock-covered toe. "You know that doesn't always change anything. Do you have friends to sit with at lunch this year?"

Rylee shook her head, the sour worm suddenly becoming too sweet and disgusting. "No."

"Sometimes in life we're just going to be alone. You can get a lot of reading done during lunch." Her mother gave a sad smile. "I'm sorry, sweetie. It can be tough finding new friends, especially at this age. It gets easier, though. Once you get used to being by yourself, you can learn how to look forward to it. You can pack yourself a really good lunch, or bring a book you've wanted to read, or use the time to make a date with yourself to do something fun, like doing a really cute manicure or learning how to needle felt. It's okay to make a date with yourself."

"I guess. I just don't get it, though!" Rylee threw up her hands, what was left of her gummy worm clenched in her fingers. "People had all this drama in the nineties when you were young—but we're so much better at everything now! I mean, we have—stuff. Technology. Phones. Self-driving cars. We should be experts at hanging out. Communicating. Friend drama is so over. People should have figured out how to do it better by now!"

Mom blinked, looking like she wanted to laugh. "Well, at least you're on trend. I mean, you're having old-school drama just like your *old*, old mother had back in the day, right?"

"I didn't mean to call you *old*," grumped Rylee. Of

course, Mom got all twisted about the unimportant part. "I just mean—it's really weird that after all this time, people can't do any better than to pull dumb pranks and be mean to each other. Everybody says friendships are supposed to be so easy, but they're *not*. How come people can't just be *nice*!? And hang out? And just—not make up lies about people, and stuff?"

"You'd be surprised," Mom said dryly. "Mean girls were practically invented in my day. There were scientific studies and a whole movie and everything. We didn't want to have all of that friendship drama Geema's generation did, but it happened. The drama is just part of growing up sometimes."

For a moment, Rylee was sure she could smell the heavy stench of chlorine and feel goose bumps ripple over her clammy skin. No, this wasn't just some growing-up drama—it wasn't like that. Mom had to be wrong.

"No," Rylee insisted. "That's . . . It isn't always like that. There has to be a reason *why* people stop being friends. There has to be something people can *do* to keep drama from starting. Don't you think someone wrote about it somewhere? I'm going to look it up."

"Well . . . that sounds like it'll take a minute," Mom said carefully. "Are you sure you're going to have time to dig into something like that on top of your school-work?"

Rylee gave a twisted half smile. "Yeah. I'll do it in the library . . . during lunch."

This time, when her mother reached out to hug her, Rylee let her.

5

Nowhere to Hide

By the second day of school, Rylee was prepared enough at homeroom that she could pretend that her vision was limited to the side of the room where Aaliyah wasn't. She was already used to Mrs. Hahn cracking jokes and giving them long lists of vocabulary words in English language arts, and when Mr. Pfister sped through the review in geometry, Rylee already knew she'd have to go back and read her hastily scribbled notes later so she'd remember everything.

By third period, Rylee was prepared for boredom, so seeing the words "What is a chorus?" written in the middle of the whiteboard in big block letters didn't even make her sigh. She found her spot on the seating chart and plopped down unenthusiastically.

"Welcome to chorus! Have any of you ever heard of a chorus that doesn't have singers?" Despite her boring question, Ms. Dowler seemed to vibrate with personality. She wore a ruffled red-and-white blouse, wide-legged beige pants with a high waist, and her tan espadrilles were embroidered with red flowers. A big red flower was tucked behind her ear.

At the mumbling response from her students, Ms. Dowler answered her own question. "I'm sure you know, a chorus is a group of musicians, usually singers! This quarter, we're going to try our hand at building a ukulele chorus! How many of you have a ukulele?"

Surprised, Rylee hesitantly held up her hand. Daddy Warren had gone on a work trip to Honolulu years ago, and brought back coffee, macadamia chocolates, and flowery shirts for Axel and Rylee. Mom and Geema had received pearls from Maui. He'd also bought himself a funny little pear-shaped ukulele.

"The salesman said it's easy to play," he had assured his wife. "We'll learn a few songs, and then you can serenade me," he had teased.

Geema had smiled, given Daddy Warren a big kiss, and handed the ukulele to Rylee a week later.

"That old man has another thought coming if he

thinks I'm going to ruin my manicure," Geema had said. "You have fun with that, honey. Play us something nice."

It had been a couple of years, and Rylee hadn't done more than learn how to tune the thing, but now she felt a tiny stirring of excitement. She'd never taken piano lessons, and the thought of playing an instrument on her own was kind of cool.

"Eight, nine . . . ten of you!" Ms. Dowler clapped her hands. "This is great! I have enough ukuleles for everyone, but as we learn ukulele songs this quarter, some of you might want to bring your own instruments from home, and that's fine. Who knows anything about the history of ukuleles?"

At the end of class, Rylee knew for one thing that Ms. Dowler had gone to school on Oahu, and the flower behind her ear was a silk plumeria, and, a third thing, that Rylee was going to have "Over the Rainbow" stuck in her head for the rest of her life. Beyond that, Rylee knew that being in chorus for elective, when they got to play instruments some of the time, might not be so bad.

Afterward, Rylee followed the crowd to the cafeteria. Like Mom had suggested, she'd prepared and packed some super delicious favorites and a book that had a scary villain in it. Hopefully she could just find a spot where she could eat and ignore everyone as she read the next chapter.

But the minute Rylee followed the line of students through the open cafeteria door, she knew she couldn't do it.

Segrest had a pretty good cafeteria; there was a salad bar and a hoagie station where people could opt out of getting a whole tray of whatever was on the menu and stick to sides. A mix of round and rectangular tables offered seating throughout the room, so there was plenty of space. No one would have bothered her, exactly. Certainly not the Spite Sisters, whom Rylee was very determinedly not seeing, sitting at their usual table between the two big windows on the right side of the room. Nobody really cared what Rylee was doing, other than the cafeteria staff, who were trying to move the lines of students through quickly. It would make total sense to find a spot, sit quietly, put in her earbuds, and no one would bug her, except she just . . . couldn't force herself to move.

Rylee was pushed to the side as the tidal wave of kids flowed past, talking about everything and nothing, discussing what they'd done over break, whining about dumb quizzes, gossiping about who was wearing what, who was sitting where, and who had a crush on whom. Aaliyah was probably one of the voices, telling everyone she was in Rylee's homeroom and that Rylee had looked scared that morning when they'd almost run into each other. Nevaeh was probably looking over and laughing because Rylee was wearing the same patchwork overalls she'd had last year, and "nobody" was wearing overalls anymore. Cherise was probably staring at her *right then.* . . .

Suddenly, there were too many people, and too many thoughts. And just like that, the past rose up like a wave of pool water and slapped her in the face.

Another breeze swirled in through the wide wooden blinds. Rylee swallowed hard as she waited in the wash of cool air, listening to the faraway voices of her classmates outdoors. She hunched further, and rubbed her arms, smelling the stench of chlorine coming from her goose-pebbled skin.

"Come on, guys." Her voice wobbled. "This isn't funny."

Another creak. Rylee dug her toes into the carpet and held her breath. Where were they hiding? Had they been laughing at her all along? Rylee winced, remembering her shaking and shimmying to get free of the wet suit. Rylee didn't care about her squishy belly rolls, or how silly she must have looked, not really. It was her bust that made her uncomfortable, the sudden arrival of new curves that year that had made her wear Mom's old T-shirt over her bathing suit top. Rylee crossed her arms over her chest and hunched her shoulders, wishing fervently that she hadn't left the shirt in a sodden pile by the pool when she'd stormed into the house.

"I need my clothes," she begged, hearing her voice fray.

Seconds went by, seconds that felt like years. On the back of her neck, a cold drip from her hair reminded her that, as she waited, it was drying into a chlorinated tangle. If Rylee didn't get something to wear and get to the bathroom to rinse it soon, the chemicals would turn her hair crunchy and horrible, and there would be nothing to do but go home on the bus with it standing up all over her head. Maybe the other girls didn't do their own hair, or they didn't know how much work it would be, if Rylee didn't get the chlorine out. Why else would they do this? Rylee could feel her face heating, her throat closing. This wasn't fair. She hadn't done anything to anyone.

"Look, you guys," Rylee began, and her voice cracked. She gulped and bowed her head as her throat squeezed.

"Give them back," Rylee whispered. The tears against her cold face nearly burned, as her composure slipped, and she crumpled at last. "Please. Give them back."

For another long moment she stood there, choking on

tears and snot and pride before the paneled door next to Nevaeh's built-in dresser squeaked open. Aaliyah, Rosario, and Nevaeh had been squished inside, while Cherise stumbled from the closet behind her. Someone lifted the mattress and shoved Rylee's clothes into her hands, while someone else slammed the closet door. With side-glances and murmurs, the girls hurried out of the room. Rylee thought someone had spoken to her, but all she could hear was a roaring in her ears.

Heart racing, Rylee found herself stumbling out the side door of the cafeteria, back into the relative quiet of the corridor, eyes stinging, her book clutched tightly. No, she wasn't going to cry again. This had to stop. She couldn't keep freaking out every time she saw them. She had to do something—

"Hey, wait!"

The voice said something else, and Rylee blinked, then turned, trying to catch her breath. The speaker was a wiry boy with fluffy, rust-colored curls and a massive paperback he was trying to wedge into his backpack.

"What?"

The boy frowned at the snap in Rylee's voice, glancing at her book. "Um, the library? I said, are you going."

"Oh." Rylee took a breath and tried to look less

hostile. "Um, yeah? I guess I could."

Without hesitation, the boy held out a card dangling from its lanyard. "Great, thanks. Could you take my pass back to Mr. Blaine? Tell him Leo forgot he had the dentist."

Rylee blinked. "Sure. No problem."

Walking thoughtfully toward the library building, Rylee studied the words "Library Pass" and the little cartoon house made of books. This was . . . good. People always sat in the library for lunch if they wanted to just hang out in peace. Rylee vaguely remembered Ms. Johnston passing out a few of these during homeroom. The next day, Rylee would request one, and she'd never have to go into the cafeteria again.

Breathing a little easier, Rylee entered the library through the plate glass doors, relieved when the sandy-haired Mr. Blaine, with his big beard and a long brown ponytail, smiled up at her from the circulation desk. "This guy named Leo—" she began, but Mr. Blaine was already on to his librarian spiel.

"Just put your pass in the box, and sign in," he said, gesturing to a clipboard on the counter. "And in case you don't remember, the rules are"—he held up a finger for each of the three—"make sure you get a drink and use the restroom, because once you're here, you're here until the bell chimes. Also, there's no food or drink in the library, no exceptions, and finally, keep the noise down to a dull roar, all right?"

"Got it," Rylee said in relief. Sitting in a corner quietly was something she could definitely do.

But the moment Rylee turned to lose herself in the magazine aisle, she heard her name.

"Hey, Rylee! I didn't know you were joining Press Club!"

6

Cranky Cowriters

DeNia—of course it was DeNia; the girl was *everywhere*—stood beaming at Rylee, the sparkly pink clip in her short curls matching her pink T-shirt. Her giant backpack luggage was not, for once, stationed right at her feet.

"Oh, hey," Rylee said weakly. She *wasn't* going to get mixed up with DeNia Alonso, no matter how broadly she was smiling. Rylee couldn't entirely ignore the surge of relief that filled her just from a friendly voice saying her name, but seriously—no.

Rylee waved and tried to step around DeNia. "Hi. I . . . was just going to read—"

"No, no, no! Come with me! Ms. Johnston's just

told us about the Junior High Press Awards. I didn't even know private schools were included in that!"

"I—wait, there's awards? For the paper?"

"Oh, yeah, it's a big deal," DeNia said, leading the way toward a nest of tables near the back of the main section of the room. "Schools can send two editions of their paper for consideration, but a teacher can nominate an individual journalist, too. Ms. Johnston said she wants to see some of us reporting on STEM issues, because that's huge right now, but I can't think of a topic, so I've been walking around."

Ms. Johnston's voice carried as voices quieted. "Folks, this is just a reminder that pitches are due next Friday—which gives you a week to work with. I'm available especially if any of you newcomers would like to talk about a piece you'd like to submit or have any questions before class tomorrow."

DeNia suddenly bounced on her toes. "I've got an idea. It's my science fair project; I don't know why I didn't think of that. It's science *plus* journalism. Come on!"

"No, I'll just—" Rylee began, but DeNia was heading for Ms. Johnston at a fast clip. Rylee trailed awkwardly behind, wishing DeNia's feelings wouldn't be hurt if she just turned around and walked away. The science fair was in *March*. How was DeNia already so hyped in September that she could write an article about it?

"My project is really cool," DeNia was saying. "I designed a game for little kids last year. They had to cooperate on a bunch of puzzles to find a code word, which they input to get into a multiplayer game online. One of the testers for the game was Mr. Gil, and he said he could have used something like that for junior high science, so that's my project this year, I think."

"Huh," Rylee said, glancing at the tables full of students that they passed—lucky, lucky people reading in *peace*. She couldn't think of anything that sounded less fun. First, she would never work for teachers in her free time. Second, making a game for junior high students to find some code word or something might be okay, but more than likely it would be seriously cringey.

The longer Rylee listened to DeNia's enthusiastic explanation of her idea, as she laid it out now for Ms. Johnston, the more Rylee wanted to just walk away.

"—and everyone will collaborate on the clues, so, besides getting the code word, everyone will get a chance to, you know, do what they're the best at— you know, some people are good readers, and some people are good at guessing, and some people will be there to sort of keep records, and everyone can kind of show off their skills. It's a cooperative learning game that's going to make people better friends, too," DeNia added.

"Um, so, DeNia?" Rylee blurted into the pause. "Is this your only idea?"

Both DeNia and Ms. Johnston turned toward her with raised brows.

"You don't think her game is going to work?" Ms. Johnston asked.

Rylee's face heated. "Sorry, no—I mean, I don't *know* if it'll work because I'm just hearing about this project, but, um . . . people are actually terrible at that, no offense," Rylee said.

"Terrible at what?" DeNia asked, her eyebrows pinched. "The kindergarten kids who played the game were great! They found the code, and they had fun, too."

Rylee winced, wishing she hadn't said anything. "Oh, sure . . . people will probably find the code just fine. I just meant that they're not going to be friends or anything. We do group projects at school because we *have* to, but none of us, like, finish and suddenly decide we're besties for all time afterward or whatever. That's all I meant, sorry." Rylee rubbed her arm awkwardly. "I really didn't mean to interrupt," she added. "Just ignore me."

"But people *can* become better friends from playing a game," DeNia insisted. "Don't you remember last year Mr. Gil telling us about this study on video games? How people doing virtual games and online stuff together helped them make new friends?"

Rylee smiled a little. "Uh, *no*. Only you remember every single science thing you hear. I'm just saying most people are kind of bad at being friends in general, and a science game isn't going to fix that. Actually, you probably shouldn't put anything about friendship in your article at all, just to be safe. I mean, nobody really knows what *makes* people friends anyway, right?"

"I do," DeNia said, sounding smug. "Spending time together. Playing *games*. Which raises people's oxytocin levels."

"Their what?" Rylee blinked.

"It's a hormone our brains make," DeNia explained. "It's what makes people bond and fall in love and stuff."

Rylee hadn't ever heard of oxytocin, which made what DeNia was saying even more annoying. "No—people don't only bond because of *hormones*. If that were true, everyone would be bonding with everyone. And I doubt a game is going to raise anyone's oxy-whatever."

"People do *everything* because of hormones," DeNia insisted. "Haven't you been paying attention to anything from science class? Hormones change people's blood sugar and their blood pressure, and how fast they grow, and their metabolism, and a bunch of other things. People are *completely* controlled by hormones."

"I said hormones aren't the *only* thing," Rylee countered. People were turning to listen. Ugh, DeNia just *had* to show off in front of a teacher. Rylee knew that hormones were a big deal—she had experienced being moody through her own body cycles—so she totally understood how powerful hormones were. Hormones were fixable, though.

Unlike friendship.

Rylee shrugged, dismissing the topic. "Fine, whatever, your game is going to release hormones and make people everywhere be best friends forever. Great! Have fun with that."

"That wasn't what I said oxytocin does," DeNia said grumpily. "You—"

"You know, this is a *really* interesting conversation," Ms. Johnston interrupted. "I'm hearing two wildly different viewpoints about friendship and science, from two writers in my fifth-period journalism class. As I recall, you two are the same two students who talked to me this morning about more time to turn in article ideas. I think you've got your idea. You two could come up with something on, oh, the science of friendship or something. Nate can make room for you in the news section, and you can share the byline to create a couple of features, even."

"I—I'm not joining Press Club, I don't think," Rylee blurted.

"That's fine," Ms. Johnston said. "You can still write together during regular class time."

"Ms. Johnston . . . I'm not sure Rylee's really serious about science," DeNia interrupted. She turned an apologetic glance to Rylee. "No offense."

"What do you mean not serious about science? I'm serious," Rylee sputtered.

DeNia looked uncomfortable. "I just mean our three pieces are worth ten percent of our quarter grade. We can't afford to mess up, or we'll have to do every other article perfectly to make more than a B minus. It's just kind of risky if you're not . . . serious."

Rylee gave DeNia an angry look. "Whatever. I won't be the one who messes up."

DeNia sighed. "I just want us to get a good grade."

"As a reminder, pitches are due next Friday for our regular journalism class," Ms. Johnston said, looking from one girl to the other. "I'm confident that *both* of you will be serious, and get these pieces turned in on time. I look forward to all of you taking those sharp minds and seeing what you can come up with."

"Science journalism," Geema repeated with a little laugh. "Well, isn't that something?"

"Sounds good," Daddy Warren said, stabbing a slice of beet from the salad bowl and dropping it on his plate. Daddy Warren didn't say much at the dinner table, usually preferring to plow steadily through the mountain of creamy potato casserole he loved, gravy-covered roast, and green salad.

Rylee shrugged and pressed the edge of her fork into a wedge of potato. "I guess. Ms. Johnston says science journalism is especially important to current events, because it's not just letting people know about scientific breakthroughs, but helping people understand what the facts are, so they can know what is and what isn't true about them."

"Listen to you, sounding so grown," Geema said again, raising her eyebrows. "Out here talking about current events and scientific breakthroughs and things."

Rylee paused with her fork full of food, eyeing her grandmother uncertainly. "It's . . . I'm not trying to sound grown, Geema. That's just what Ms. Johnston said."

Geema patted Rylee's hand, immediately looking less amused. "I know, sweet, I know. You go out there and do your reporting and make us proud."

"Of course, she will," Daddy Warren said loyally. "We're always proud of our girl."

Rylee made herself smile and take a bite. Later, after dinner, she was going to get on Face2Face with DeNia and they were going to work on making a pitch for Ms. Johnston's stupid journalism assignment. It was too bad DeNia hadn't just taken her advice—the game actually sounded pretty interesting if she would have taken the friendship part out of it—

"—Grace's granddaughter reporting on?"

Uh-oh, Rylee had tuned out while she ate, just like Daddy Warren did. "I'm sorry, Geema, can you repeat that?"

"I asked what Ms. Grace's granddaughter was reporting on?"

Oh no. Rylee took a deep breath, dread filling her lungs like a dense fog. Grace Shabazz was Geema's oldest, dearest friend who she'd been friends with since they had met at a church picnic in the third grade. Ms. Grace was also Aaliyah Washington's grandma.

"Oh, um, Aaliyah isn't reporting—she took a different elective. She's in culinary arts. Again." Rylee's voice was pitched too high.

Her grandmother's generous mouth turned down in dismay. "Hold up now—what happened to you all taking that cooking class together?"

Rylee hesitated, then told the truth . . . with certain facts edited. "There's only so much room in each elective," she said. "Not everybody can have their first choice."

"But that isn't fair! You girls ought to have had first pick, since you took that cooking class last year," Geema said, and jabbed the air with her finger. "Someone ought to speak to that cooking teacher of yours. She—"

"No! No, no, no," Rylee blurted. "Geema, we're not allowed to complain. We're supposed to be, um, mature this year," Rylee added, waving her hands vaguely. "We're eighth graders now. Nobody can talk to her. Adults aren't supposed to get involved."

"*What!?*"

"Now, that's just good sense," Daddy Warren said approvingly. "Young folks have got to learn to work things out themselves. I like that." Daddy Warren looked at Geema, whose lips were pressed thin with affront. "Don't fuss about it, Regina. You already taught her to cook."

Thank goodness for Daddy Warren. Rylee breathed a sigh of relief.

"I know she can cook—that's not the point, Warren," Geema said, throwing up her hands. "I didn't sign up not to interfere if something's going on at that school that I don't like. This is ridiculous. Rylee had fun with her little friends in that cooking class last year. All this science journalism and current events reporting sounds so . . . serious. She doesn't need to be so serious when she's so young."

"It's fine, Geema," Rylee said, soothing her grand-mother's ruffled temper. "I promise, journalism is okay. And anyway, Aaliyah's in my homeroom class. I see her first thing every morning. It's fine."

"Not allowed to complain, my *foot*," Geema mut-tered, going back to her plate. "I have never heard something so ridiculous in my *life*."

The text popped up onto Rylee's laptop screen, and she groaned. She and DeNia had planned to get online that night and talk, but Rylee had found herself putting it off. DeNia was bound to come up with a few more sci-ence things she hadn't heard of—oxy-whatever—and then she'd lord her science knowledge over Rylee like she was the only one who knew anything. Rylee wondered if talking to Ms. Johnston would do any good. Couldn't she get out of this? At the very least, couldn't she get out of doing it with DeNia?

Rylee tapped the green icon on her screen and managed to find a weak smile as DeNia's face moved into view. "Hey, DeNia."

"Hey. Hi." DeNia was wearing a patterned scarf, and she looked . . . nervous. Rylee felt a sudden surge of empathy. This must be really weird for DeNia, too. Rylee wasn't the only one Ms. Johnston had shoved into this partnership.

"Cute scarf," Rylee said, hoping she sounded kind. "I love that wrap style."

"Oh. Thanks." DeNia's hand hovered briefly near her head. "It's my mom's."

"Cool," Rylee said. "Uh . . . so we're supposed to write something about friendship."

"And science," DeNia added.

"Yeah. I mean, I guess that's what she said, but I don't see how this is going to work," Rylee said, hearing the exasperation in her voice. "I don't know enough about science to make this work. I mean, I *did* listen in science class, and I got a B last year," Rylee added, to make sure DeNia knew she could do the work. "I still don't get this."

DeNia nodded. "I'm not sure what Ms. Johnston wants, either, but . . . why don't we just do two sides of an argument? Like, I think hormones make people feel good about having friends, and you think . . ." DeNia paused.

"I think that, too," Rylee protested. "I remember now—people feel good when they get compliments from their friends, and hormones are what do that, which makes you be nicer or whatever, so you get more compliments. I just don't think it would work in a game, that's all.

"Plus, people our age are still growing. Aren't our hormones changing all the time or something? I just don't think you can say our hormones are making us friends. Or else some people's hormones really, *really* aren't working right."

DeNia shrugged. "Okay, that's fair. That seems like something we can write about."

Rylee rubbed the side of her forehead. This was not going well. "No, we *can't* write about that," she said patiently. "I'm not going to look stupid for disagreeing with science while you pull out some more hormones or something else you know about. I need some time to research." Rylee brightened as the idea developed. "Yeah—we both need to do some research and come up with stuff to base our arguments on. Then we'll, um, figure out which ones we want to use, and *then* we'll write the article."

"Okay, but that's adding steps," DeNia warned her. "We still have to pitch this, Ms. Johnston has to approve it, then we have to *write* it, and Nate Tan, the news editor this quarter, will check it over and get it back to us if we have errors or whatever. Don't forget we have to write our three pieces a month for journalism class, and this one still counts for our grade. We have to make it good, and we only have three weeks."

"It's going to be good," Rylee assured her confidently. "Just let me get some research—and then we can start to collaborate. It'll be fine."

Rylee was watching a video of a two-year-old girl attempting a K-pop dance routine when a repeated thump against her door let her know her brother was home—and had found a ball somewhere.

Sighing mightily, Rylee yanked off her headphones. "Axel! Cut it out!" she yelled.

The thumping continued. Resigned, she rolled off the bed and flung open the door to find her brother sitting in the doorway of his room, rolling a spiky rubber stress ball across the narrow hall space.

Rylee stopped the little orb with her foot, resisting the urge to stomp on it and feel the satisfying squish. "Other people just *knock* when they want something, you know."

"I *am* knocking," Axel said, smiling sweetly and gesturing for her to give him the ball.

Rylee nudged the ball with her foot and sat down on the floor, eyes narrowed on her brother's face. He was laughing at her about something, the little snot.

Trying to channel her inner peace, Rylee took a deep breath. "Fine. You knocked, I answered. What do you want?"

"*Nada*, Hermana," Axel singsonged, rolling the ball back to her.

Ugh. Rylee swatted the ball back, hard. Even though he was picking up Spanish fast in his sixth-grade language elective, with everything else, her brother was a disaster. His shirt was two sizes too big, and there was a smear of chocolate—or something—around his mouth. He hardly paid attention to anything but his computer, and Rylee couldn't imagine how he had any friends—though he was always meeting them online, so they must not mind hanging out with the crumb-covered slob that he was. Mom always reminded her that someday her little brother would change and surprise her. Until then, he was just a big-headed pain in her behind.

Rylee tried to be calm. "Axel . . . look, am I supposed to guess what you want? Is that it?"

"*I* don't want anything," Axel said with a little smile. He rolled the ball toward her.

Rylee slapped it back, imagining smacking words out of her brother's stubborn head. "Axel, come *on*," she groaned. "If you didn't want anything, you'd be playing Wizard 1000 or whatever and not bugging me. Just *use your words*, please?"

"It's Wizard101, and I'm not bugging you. I'm 'hanging out.'" Axel somehow managed to give the words air quotes as he sent back the ball and smirked again. "Like Geema said to."

Rylee stopped the ball, feeling her nails dig into the squishy, nubbly surface as her hand tensed. "Wait, wait, *wait*. Are you saying Geema sent you to *play with me?*"

Axel nodded, making *gimme* motions toward the ball. "Yep. Said to make myself useful."

Rylee sputtered. "*What!?* Why? Axel, tell me *exactly* what Geema said."

Axel raised his eyes to the ceiling and imitated his grandmother's voice. "'Jayna, did you know your daughter can't even be with her friends at school?' and Mom said, 'What are you talking about?' and Geema said, 'I'm talking about that poor child not getting into her cooking class. Why didn't you call the school and fix this?' and then Mom said, 'Mama, there's nothing that needs to be fixed, and the only way out of some problems is to go through—'"

"Oh *no*." Rylee lunged up in a tangle of arms and legs and ran down the hall.

"Wait—give me the ball!" Axel yelled after her.

Rylee flung it in her brother's direction and hoped it popped him upside his hard head. Ugh, this was all his fault. If Axel had just *knocked* on the door like a normal person and gotten to the point, she could have . . . done something sooner. Given Mom a sign that she wasn't supposed to talk to Geema about her "problems." What if Geema had already called her friend Grace? What if they were going to try and . . . *do* something!? Rylee loved her grandmother with all her heart, but Geema's help was sometimes *the absolute worst*.

When Rylee skidded into the kitchen, she knew she was too late. Geema turned to her from her seat at the kitchen table with a martial light in her eye.

"Rylee, why didn't you tell me about Grace's grand-daughter?"

"Tell you what?" Rylee asked, shooting her mother a frantic look. "There's nothing to tell . . . or say . . . or whatever." Rylee twisted her fingers in the hem of her T-shirt.

"Well, that's not what your mother says," Geema said, bristling.

Rylee's stomach knotted. "Mom?"

Her mother put an arm around her waist and squeezed in a sideways hug. "Calm down, Rylee. I just mentioned you girls had grown apart, and your grand-mother has decided that means she needs to call Grace and get everyone together for a little playdate." Mom frowned at Geema. "And, Mama, I'm saying again, for the record—they're too old for that mess, and you need to leave the girls alone to work things out—or not—by themselves. They're young ladies now."

"And *I* am saying again, for the record, that I don't see the harm in putting in a little effort to try and keep a friend. Rylee, I've got an extra ticket to a musi-cal Ms. Grace and I are going to see on Sunday night. I thought you could go with us, and then we could meet Miss Aaliyah afterward and have a bite somewhere and see if we can't mend some fences."

"What? NO," blurted Rylee. At her grandmother's sharp look, Rylee improvised quickly. "I mean, no *thank you*, Geema. I can't—I'm going to, um, somebody's house in the afternoon to work on a journalism project. We're all supposed to write three stories, and they're worth ten percent of our grade."

"See?" Rylee's mother said, bending to press a kiss to her mother's cheek. "Rylee's got new friends she's hanging out with, so everything's taken care of. Why don't you and Ms. Grace go to your musical, and let Daddy use that extra ticket?"

"Oh, your father doesn't want to go to any musical," Geema said, waving a hand. "Rylee, if you don't want to go, that's fine. But you should take my advice anyway. You two girls ought to sit down and talk. Ms. Grace and I haven't managed to remain friends all these long years by letting little things come between us. Fussing with each other is part of friendship. Good friends talk to each other and work things out."

"I know, Geema," Rylee mumbled, flexing her sock-clad toes against the wooden kitchen floor. She wanted to laugh. Little things.

Rylee bolted into her clothes, hiccuping and shivering as she twisted and shoved her goose-bumped arms and

71

legs into her shorts and T-shirt. She wedged her toes into her flip-flops and ran for the front door, her duffel banging her hip.

"Rylee?" Mrs. Green asked as she raced past. "Was that Rylee Swanson?"

Even in the warmth of the kitchen, Rylee found herself shivering helplessly and rubbed her arms.

No. What happened would *never* be little.

The *Segrest Sentinel* Reports

Friendship: Why Scientists Study It
by DeNia Alonso

***

As part of the activities of Press Club, this year eighth graders DeNia Alonso and Rylee Swanson are conducting a scientific journalism project about friendship. Throughout the semester, they will be reporting on different aspects of friendship and how it affects those of us in junior high.

***

Some friendships don't just make you feel good—they can make you healthier.

Dr. Sheldon Cohen, of Carnegie Mellon University and the University of Pittsburgh School of Medicine, reported that friendships can lower our stress and make it less likely that we will catch colds.

Researchers discovered that physical signs of good health were more present in people with good friendships. While that doesn't mean that having good friendships means you'll automatically never get sick, it does show that the two things are often linked together and may have been part of survival in early human societies (Cohen et al. 1940–1).

If friendships lowering the chances of you spending a week sneezing seems surprising, keep reading. There's more:

A scientific study in the *Journal of Happiness Studies* followed one thousand students in New Zealand for thirty-two years. Scientists interviewed the students periodically from elementary school to adulthood and found out that people who were connected to friends as adolescents were more successful adults. Even if they didn't do that well in school, if they had good friends, they did better in life, were more successful, and they felt happier—they reported feeling satisfied with their lives (Olsson et al. 1071).

What makes these two studies alike? They both show why studying friendship is significant and help to answer the question of how it can affect all of us.

Science finds answers for everyday problems by asking the right questions. That's why science studies friendships. By asking the right questions and finding out why the answers matter, we can make our friendships—and our lives—even better.

Works Cited

Cohen, Sheldon, et al. "Social Ties and Susceptibility to the Common Cold." *Journal of the American Medical Association*, vol. 277, no. 24, 1997, pp. 1940-4.

Olsson, Craig A., et al. "A 32-Year Longitudinal Study of Child and Adolescent Pathways to Well-Being in Adulthood." *Journal of Happiness Studies*, vol. 14, 2013, pp. 1069-83.

The *Segrest Sentinel* Reports
Sidebar: Who, What & Why

***

As part of the activities of Press Club,
this year eighth graders DeNia Alonso and
Rylee Swanson are conducting a scientific
journalism project about friendship. Here
we learn a bit more about them.

***

D E N I A • A L O N S O

**Q: WHO are you? How do you describe
yourself?**

A: *I'm curious, friendly, a hard worker, and
a good friend. I like music, puzzles, and
games. I like to know how things work and
to figure out if they can work better.*

Q: WHAT is friendship to you?

A: *Friendship is people looking out for
each other and getting together to create
or work for things together that they
couldn't do alone.*

Q: WHY are you interested in reporting on friendship?

A: *I'm interested in the way science works in everything. I like to invent games, and I read somewhere that games are a good way for people to make friends. I would like to know how that is possible and what other things can affect friendship.*

R Y L E E • S W A N S O N

Q: WHO are you? How do you describe yourself?

A: *I like art, clothes, cooking, riding my bike, and a bunch of other stuff, depending on who I'm with and what I'm in the mood for.*

Q: WHAT is friendship to you?

A: *Friendship is supporting people and having their backs. It's knowing things about someone and keeping them a secret without gossiping.*

Q: WHY are you interested in reporting on friendship?

A: *I'm interested in friendship research because if we can use science, we might be better at figuring out the people we're friends with and how to be better at being friends.*

Friendship isn't a simple idea. Everyone has a different idea about what it is and about how it works. The authors of this article, DeNia and Rylee, partnered to work on a project in journalism class. Does working together with a friend make you closer friends? Or will your friendship survive?

What about social media friends? DeNia usually clicks the heart next to actress Faeri Williams's posts on BytReels. When you "like" someone's social media post, or "follow" them, what does that mean for friendship? Does it mean anything?

How long do you have to "hang out" with someone before a friendship is real?

If you've ever had questions like this, keep reading. The Segrest School Friendship Study is our way to use science to help us find answers.

7

Research Realizations

"Okay, so, I found data for our journalism article," DeNia said as she walked into homeroom the next morning, slinging her massive gray backpack off her shoulder in between their desks.

That day DeNia's short hair was half covered with a red Rosie the Riveter bandana to match her sleeveless red top and the red patches on her dark blue jeans. It was a shame an outfit so cute was wasted on someone so annoying.

"You found . . . data?" Rylee said in disbelief as DeNia unloaded a waxed canvas lunch bag, a shoebox, a striped pencil box, and a stack of color-coded folders. The girl must have muscles like a weight lifter to carry so much stuff.

"Yep. I went online last night and found some amazing articles," DeNia said, opening yet another folder and pulling out a stapled stack of papers.

"And you . . . printed them?" Rylee blinked. There were over twenty pages, and Rylee winced as she eyed the stack. "Couldn't you have saved a few trees and texted me some links?"

"No, I could not have," DeNia said stiffly, beginning to repack her massive gray pack. "First, Mom says it's better to read research materials in hard copy, and she should know, since she's a biologist and she reads tons of research. Second, you probably don't have access to the journals my mom reads. You have to pay for them."

"Oh," Rylee said, feeling stupid. Since *her* mother worked in a human resources department, she guessed that made DeNia's mom the expert.

"We have to write up a pitch for the piece, and Ms. Johnston has to approve it," DeNia was explaining again.

"I already *know* we have to pitch the article, but today? We don't even have journalism today," Rylee protested, feeling the familiar buzz of irritation riding her nerves at DeNia's pushiness. "It's Friday. We have a whole seven days before we have to turn this in!"

"That doesn't mean we can't work on it." DeNia shoved the shoebox back into the depths of her pack and zipped it away. "You can sit next to me in advisory."

Rylee rolled her eyes. Unlike when they were seventh graders and it was a short, once-a-month thing, advisory was now just like a regular class. Students would meet with their homeroom groups twice a week to do art and service projects and talk with the co-teachers, who took turns leading the group. It was supposed to be all about self-expression and getting to know everyone, so there wasn't a syllabus or anything she could do to study ahead. Worst of all, there were no assigned seats.

Since finding out Aaliyah was in her homeroom, Riley had been low-key dreading the whole thing, and now DeNia was making it worse.

"I might not get to sit next to you," she reminded DeNia. "And we might have to, you know, pay attention in class or whatever?"

"Fine, don't worry about it," DeNia whispered as Ms. Johnston turned on the wall monitor, and the announcements music began to play. "It'll get done."

Rylee opened her mouth to answer and met Ms.

Johnston's eagle eye. Giving DeNia an annoyed glance she didn't notice, Rylee flipped through the stack of papers. She caught a word here and there like "neuro" something and "prairie voles" and . . . these weren't magazines. Rylee scanned the bottoms of a few pages and read off the titles. *Young Minds in Science. Neuron.* The *Journal of the American Medical Association.* Yeah, she definitely didn't subscribe to these kinds of magazines. She went back to the stack from *Young Minds in Science* and opened it.

Scientists in Southern California had a group of girls play an online game of catch . . . wearing scanners on their heads that read their brain waves!? Rylee's eyebrows jumped up. That actually sounded cool.

The game was kind of like catch, and each player in the group got a turn . . . or, most of them did. Sometimes, the throwers would just leave certain people out.

Rylee frowned, reading the small, printed words slowly. The people who got left out of the game of catch were left out on purpose—it wasn't catch; it was keep-away. The people excluded over and over again, the scientists discovered, had parts of their brain get active—the same parts that other scientists had discovered became active when people hurt themselves physically. Further studies had revealed that insults were also something that made the body react like it had felt a literal slap. Another study about social isolation had even more details about damage, pointing out that social isolation and being lonely could be as bad for the body as smoking fifteen cigarettes a day!

That . . . was *amazing*. And weird. And . . . Rylee felt her forehead bunching as she pondered. When the Spite Sisters had . . . well, when they'd been *spiteful* toward her, and she'd felt like she'd gotten punched in the face . . . that pain had been real? As real as breaking her arm would have been?

Whoa.

Rylee found herself imagining everyone's brains lighting up with every feeling they had. How many other brains at Segrest were, at any time of the day, flashing signals of sadness and loneliness, of feeling stuck and alone on some way-out-there island in the middle of the ocean of school friendships?

Rylee really wished she knew why she was the only one on her island.

As it turned out, Rylee had plenty of time to consider the question in advisory. She had walked into Ms. Johnston's classroom and instead of the calm order of morning homeroom, she was confronted with chaos: desks clustered in groups throughout the room, each covered with butcher paper or plastic, bins of colorful paper, buttons and yarn, glue, and other items. The science teacher who was Ms. Johnston's advisory co-teacher, Mr. Gil, gave Rylee an elbow bump—his usual hands-free greeting—and pointed Rylee to the whiteboard for instructions.

Throughout advisory, the words on the whiteboard had stayed in mile-high letters.

Who are you? Who am I? I want my self-portrait to convey these three key ideas about myself: I am _____, _____, and _____.

The "Who am I?" part of the question made Rylee sigh. Teachers always asked things like that, and she never knew what to say.

"There are lots of ways you can answer the question," Ms. Johnston had said as she urged people into seats. "You'll have all semester to work on your portrait, but you'll need to answer the Question of the Day today and share those three key ideas about yourself. What makes you especially . . . you?"

Rylee dropped her backpack at a nearby desk and

dithered over the plastic bins of supplies. Art sometimes felt so complicated—Rylee just wanted to make something pretty, but Ms. Johnston had already said this was supposed to be about *her.*

"This would be easier if we could have spray paint," a boy in a burgundy sweatshirt was suggesting to Ms. Johnston.

"Well, I can't give you spray paint, but I do have graffiti markers!" Ms. Johnston held up a packet of fat pens, and a couple of students rose happily to grab some. Rylee shook her head as the boy offered the box to her. She still wasn't sure enough about what she was doing.

Rylee eventually took two sheets of black paper and a few sheets of blue, a handful of coffee stirrers, and some scissors. She concentrated on cutting the paper into thin strips. If nothing else, the blue and black were the colors of her hair with its extensions. Maybe she could make a braid or an origami bookmark like everyone had made in the fourth grade. That, at least, was kind of a decent "key idea" start, or at least one of the three she was supposed to find. She was . . . a lot of things, folded into one person. Nobody could argue with that, right?

"Hey—are you going to use all of those stir sticks?"

"Uh . . . I don't think so. Here." Rylee handed the handful of narrow wooden stirrers to the girl next to her, who had taken white glue and twine and smeared it into a kind of sculpted body. Rylee figured the buttons on the table were going to be eyes, and the stir sticks might be spindly arms and legs. Rylee gave a polite smile, wondering what key ideas about the girl would be shown in her art—maybe that she liked *Coraline*? Or watching cheesy horror movies?

On a large sheet of black poster board taped to the wall in the back of the classroom, Mr. Gil was using chalk. He wasn't sketching a person, though— his self-portrait was a . . . dog? The big, pointed ears, round dark eyes, and worried-looking little face came together to create the beginnings of an adorably big-headed Chihuahua.

More people than Rylee noticed, and some commented, saying it looked like their dog, or wondering aloud how a dog represented their science teacher. The hair on the back of Rylee's neck rose, however, when she heard, "That is *so* cute, Mr. Gil," from a familiar voice.

Rylee turned and pretended it was only coincidence that had her looking toward Aaliyah, who was also working with twine. She was braiding it and putting beads along the braid—making it look a lot like her hair. Rylee's lips tightened. If Aaliyah was making a doll, it wouldn't be spooky or anything. It would be super cute, like just about everything Aaliyah did.

Rylee realized she'd stopped cutting and had wound a strip of paper around her finger so tightly that her finger was throbbing.

"Why don't you try using a paintbrush handle for that?" Ms. Johnston suggested, dropping a couple of thin brushes on Rylee's desk. "That will save your poor fingers, and you can get the quill spirals a bit tighter, too."

"Oh . . ." Rylee blinked to attention. "Um, thanks."

She'd seen paper quill art on display once when she and Mom had gone to the big central library branch downtown. Winding strips of paper into spirals seemed like a pretty good idea for a self-portrait. Maybe she would make a stick figure with a big head . . . crammed full of tight spirals of pink paper. There was another key idea about her—there was too much chaos going on inside her head.

Rylee had a nest of curled paper on the top of her desk when DeNia swept past and dropped a sheet of paper on Rylee's desk.

In a hasty motion, Rylee automatically slid the paper

beneath her work, only peeping at a corner of it a few minutes later when Mr. Gil and Ms. Johnston continued to appear busy in different parts of the room.

Rylee leaned closer and frowned at the lines of closely crammed print. It looked like an assignment . . . ?

Wait, no!

Rylee hurried up to the art supply bins, then subtly drifted over to where DeNia was choosing from a bin full of what looked like broken pieces of watches, springs, gears, and washers.

"You wrote the pitch!" Rylee whispered furiously. "We're supposed to do it together."

"You're welcome," DeNia whispered, plunging her hands into a bin of sequins in all sizes. She chose a handful of black ones. "If we get the article approved today, we can do the writing next week. Easy, right?"

Rylee felt panicky. "We haven't agreed on anything," she protested. "I'm still reading the stuff you brought me, but I haven't had time to research!"

DeNia shrugged. "You can find your own research if you want. We can do interviews even. We just have to make a decision and start *something*, Rylee. Ms. Johnston said to do something, so we need to do it. Trust me, the proposal's the easy part."

Easy? None of this was easy! Speechless, Rylee

snatched another piece of art paper and stalked back to her desk.

DeNia Alonso was a mistake. The girl whose brain had downloaded and saved everyone's science fair projects since forever wasn't someone Rylee could work with. This whole project was going to be way too stressful. They hadn't even started working and DeNia had already taken over! This was going to be a nightmare.

Across the room, Aaliyah laughed. Rylee found herself turning, then forced herself back to the proposal in front of her.

Topic/Fact: Junior high friendships end, often. Most friendships won't last through high school.

Explanation/Evidence: Use studies about friendship to create Segrest Survey. Ask eighth graders about how their friendships have changed since grade six. Potential topics: Ask about new friendships in seventh or eighth grade. Ask about losing friends. Ask what makes a bad friend. Ask what makes a good friend. (Five to seven questions ONLY, if it is too long no one will finish.)

Rylee's sour stomach slowly stopped its rinse-cycle
swish and twist. This . . . proposal wasn't . . . terrible.
Maybe it wasn't what Rylee would have come up with,
but since she hadn't come up with *anything* . . .

It was actually pretty interesting that DeNia's fact
was that junior high friendships *ended*. That wasn't the
type of paper article anyone would expect. But the
facts spoke for themselves—Rylee had been in friendships since sixth grade that were over now, probably
forever.

Still, the idea that *most* junior high friendships didn't
make it all the way through high school . . . didn't
seem right. Rylee frowned, thinking about Ms. Grace,
Geema's closest friend, who had known her since she
was nine. They had grown up together, worked in the
same department store, and had both married within
the same year. They'd moved to different towns for

a while, each of them packing up and following their husbands' jobs, but eventually, they'd ended up back in the same place, and still best friends.

According to Geema, that friendship had pulled them through everything. But that couldn't be true. How could Geema be BFFs with one person for fifty years or something without having a fight? How did they keep that extra *F*?

Rylee pulled out her pencil and scribbled on the edge of the proposal.

Quotes / Additional Information / Reasoning:
Interview old/adult people. Get quotations on
what makes old friends still friends.

Rylee nodded to herself, looking down at the proposal. *Now* she was onboard.

8

Not Just a Nerd

Rylee was trying—and failing—to tune the *E* string on her ukulele the next afternoon when her mother knocked sharply on her doorframe.

"Ry, are you expecting me to drop you off at your friend's place this afternoon?"

Rylee twisted the tuner another millimeter. "Huh?"

"Your science friend? You were going over to work on something?"

What friend? Rylee blinked slowly, then shot up from bed, remembering. "Oh! Um, DeNia!"

Her mother gave her an amused look. "I was just going to run your brother to the park, so I thought

I'd see if you were ready to go. I'd rather drop you off than have you relying on buses this afternoon. You know how bad the weekend schedule is."

Rylee winced. She'd forgotten all about her fake study date. She didn't have any idea where DeNia was, or if she'd gone away for the weekend. And where *was* home for her, anyway? She and her giant backpack had to commute between her parents' houses.

"Sure. I—just a minute." Rylee began searching for her shoes.

"You have time to wash your face and change that shirt to something without a stain in the middle," Mom said, giving Rylee's clothes a once-over.

"I'll change my whole outfit," Rylee said, frowning at her cutoff sweats. "I wasn't thinking when I got dressed."

Mom pulled the door closed as Rylee dove across the bed to grab her phone. Her classmates left contact information on the junior high private pages, and Rylee was relieved to find a number for DeNia.

Answer, answer, answer, Rylee chanted internally as she texted.

Rylee: It's Rylee. Are you home? Are you busy?

An ellipsis showed DeNia was typing.

DeNia: Community center. What's up?

Rylee: Want to meet to talk about the journalism project more?

DeNia: Can do. Palm Tree Café in thirty?

Rylee gave a thumbs-up in response and sighed in relief.

The Palm Tree Café was two blocks from school, right across from the Palm Avenue branch of the public library, and next door to the park and the splashy remodeled community center. Rylee wondered briefly what DeNia had been doing there, but there was always something going on there on a weekend, like senior center art shows and quilt shows that Ms. Grace dragged Geema to see.

Rylee didn't see DeNia at any of the tables in the café when she stood in the doorway. She wasn't standing and reading the chalked menu that took up a whole wall, nor was she lingering at the condiment counter, adding rough brownish chunks of sugar to a hot drink, or getting a fat straw for bubble tea. Rylee was about to turn around and go back outside when she saw DeNia come out through the curtained door behind the counter, ducking around the short door toward a table near the back, where her backpack was wedged against the wall. Rylee let out a relieved breath and hurried her way. DeNia was wearing a cropped wrap-around cardigan and black pants that flared out around her ankles. Her shoes were weird, puffy booties.

"Are those . . . slippers?" Rylee asked, looking at the strange footwear with a disbelieving laugh. "Are you in your pajamas?"

DeNia followed Rylee's glance at her shoes, then laughed. "Hah, no. Well, they're kind of slippers," she said, and shrugged. "They're warm-up booties. I put them on after my dance group so my muscles cool down slowly."

"Hey, Dee, did you want a sandwich with this?" A café worker with a big Afro and a brightly striped apron set a cup of something hot and savory-smelling on the table and bumped her hip gently against DeNia's.

"I've got a cheese bagel in the toaster," DeNia said, smiling. "Thank you, Aunt Birdie. Rylee, did you order?"

"Uh . . . not yet," Rylee said, bewildered. Dance group? Aunts? She glanced at the lady who was bustling between the other tables, smiling and talking to the people enjoying their tea and sandwiches. DeNia wasn't only the science nerd with the massive backpack Rylee had imagined her to be at *all*. "I'll, um, go look at the menu."

"Get the soup of the day," DeNia suggested. "Auntie

Etta invented this Thai-style spicy soup, and it's really good."

"Uh, okay," Rylee said. She wandered to the menu wall, sneaking quick glances around the busy café as she did so. It was strange that the place she was familiar with was apparently totally different for DeNia. Who was Auntie Etta, anyway?

Rylee ordered the soup and a soft pretzel, which didn't exactly go, but she was overwhelmed with too many choices. She was grateful when she came back to the table to see DeNia digging in her enormous backpack, as usual.

"I can't believe you drag that big old bag around on the weekend, too," she teased.

"Where else am I supposed to put my things?" DeNia asked practically, pulling out a binder and a package of sticky notes. "Anyway, I have to have it all the time. That way, I don't ever forget my stuff at home, or at my dad's house."

"Yeah, but it's *huge*," Rylee said, sinking into the chair across the table from DeNia's and setting down her own backpack. "I mean, last week you had shoes in there. You do have a closet, don't you? A house?" Rylee joked.

DeNia's scowl was immediate. "I need my dance

shoes three times a week. Just because I'm *organized* doesn't mean I don't have a closet," she added, sounding a little annoyed. "Also, jokes about people who are unhoused are super rude."

"I was kidding," Rylee backtracked quickly, feeling the friend-positive vibes she'd been trying for slide rapidly into the negative. "I didn't know you had dance classes. Is it ballet or something?"

"No. Tap." DeNia pulled the binder toward her. She opened it, then looked up, clearly finished with anything personal. "Okay. So, did you finish reading all the articles I copied for you? Did you bring them?"

Rylee hesitated, feeling dismissed. "Uh, yeah. I brought the notes. And I read them, but—I actually started looking for something else. You know how that one study you found was about how people's brains react to being, um, rejected?" Rylee riffled through the stack of papers, enthusiasm speeding her words. "What if—what if we looked at the brains of the people who are doing the rejecting? I did get online, but I haven't found anything yet. Maybe—"

"Wait, that doesn't make sense," DeNia interrupted, her brow furrowing.

Rylee blinked. "What?"

"It doesn't make sense, researching other brains.

Why would we do that? What does it have to do with our project?"

"Why? Because—because it's interesting. I mean, don't you think so?" Rylee gestured wordlessly. "I mean—I read some more stuff about brain science, and how people's brains light up all the time, when they're mad or sad or rejected or whatever. I just thought . . . it sounded interesting," she finished weakly.

"Sure," DeNia said, unconvincingly. "But here's the thing. We already have a topic, Rylee. I've already turned it in, and Ms. Johnston will probably approve it first thing on Monday. We're writing about friendships *ending*, not about mean people's brains. How could we even track people's brain activity? And even if we found volunteers and scientists or whatever, how would we get it all done before the *Sentinel* deadline? We have, like, two weeks after pitches are due, and Ms. Johnston said our assignment is worth ten percent of our grade. We have to focus."

Just then a tall, full-bodied woman with a towering waterfall of locs set a bowl of soup and a couple of plates on the table. She dusted off her hands on her apron as Rylee murmured a polite thank-you.

DeNia gave the woman an exuberant hug and sang out, "Thanks, Auntie Etta."

"Who's your friend?" Ms. Etta asked, beaming at Rylee.

"This is Rylee—she's in my journalism class. I'm supposed to be working with her because she's new to the paper," DeNia explained.

Rylee tried to smile at DeNia's aunt while struggling not to take DeNia's criticism personally.

"Look, I can focus," Rylee said, as the woman returned to the kitchen. "I get it about the research. I just thought it was something we could add—you know, dig into, but you're right. We're doing the thing on friendships ending."

"Yeah," DeNia said, ripping off a piece of bagel. "If you want to do something to help, you could find some more articles about that—about the biology or chemistry of friendships or something. Or you can research a good way for us to get other people involved. I thought we could use an app like Good Question to make a survey that the whole school could answer or something. There's a bunch of research that still needs to be done. I can give you a whole list."

Rylee sighed. DeNia would let her "help" with this project . . . but it was DeNia's project. Not Rylee's. Rylee got that loud and clear. "Yeah, okay," she muttered.

Rylee ate her soup quietly, surprised by the sharp, sour, spicy flavors of lemongrass, coconut milk, rice, and basil. She munched on her pretzel as DeNia waved to new people who came in, getting up once or twice to go over to other tables to give hugs and talk. Rylee felt like she was a character in a play who didn't have any lines. She didn't know what or how to say this to DeNia, who had so many friends of all ages, and who tap-danced and had cool relatives who could cook. Instead of staying in the mental box that Rylee had given her, labeled Science Nerd, DeNia had danced her way out to talk to everyone and seemed to be bouncier and brighter every time she got up, calling hellos, and waving.

Rylee finally pulled out her phone, looking at the menu wall to see if she could find a Wi-Fi password. She'd intended to do some work but found herself opening a game. Throwing things at birds wasn't research, exactly, but she didn't know what else to do while DeNia socialized, and she was feeling resentful and a little sorry for herself. Even DeNia—extra, awkward, nerdy DeNia—had plenty of friends.

Rylee wondered once again if she could talk to Ms. Johnston about doing this friendship article by herself. Even though she didn't know what she'd write about, it would still be better than having DeNia veto all her suggestions before she'd even explained them all the way.

Rylee looked up as DeNia finally made her way back to the table, this time carrying a muffin that smelled deliciously of honey and basil.

"Do you want to order something else?" she asked, plopping back into her seat. "Auntie Etta just pulled these out of the oven, and they're still hot."

"That muffin's as big as your head," Rylee said, and rolled her eyes as DeNia took a big bite. "That's a *lot* of food, DeNia. I couldn't eat a whole one by myself."

"I can," DeNia said, peeling away the muffin paper for another bite. "And I'm not even embarrassed. When I get done with tap for the day, I am *starving*."

And now Rylee was being mean and judgy about food. "I don't think you should be embarrassed," Rylee sputtered, trying to backpedal. "I just meant, it's just too big for *me*, so I don't want one."

DeNia shrugged. "Your loss," she said, taking a big bite. "It's so *good*."

Ugh, and Rylee really wanted a muffin, too, but no, she'd said she didn't, and now she had to live with that, or look even sillier. *Ugh!* She didn't like this—it felt like everything she said around DeNia was wrong. Why had she wanted to meet her this afternoon anyway? Oh yeah, she *hadn't*. She just hadn't wanted Geema to think she had no friends and needed to go to a musical with her and Ms. Grace.

Even Geema thought she was pathetic. This was embarrassing. But just because she told her mom she had to meet DeNia didn't mean she had to stay. Rylee bounced to her feet.

"Well, I should go," she told DeNia. DeNia, happily involved with her muffin, nodded.

"Tomorrow," she said around a mouthful of food. "Talk to you then."

Leaving the café was a relief, but Rylee didn't want to go home just yet. She crossed the street and walked up the tree-lined walkway to the library. Whisking through the automatic doors, Rylee wandered toward the periodicals, checked out the new magazines, and meandered into the stacks. Eventually she chose a book from the teen section and crashed onto a cushion in a corner to read for a while, until two younger girls with unicorn backpacks distracted her. Rylee watched them for a moment, smiling wryly as she watched them watching others walking by. They sat in their own little bestie bubble, and they had something to say about just about everyone.

Rylee remembered what that was like. Sitting with her girls before school started, or in the cafeteria, had been like that. It had felt . . . exclusive, like Aaliyah telling them what she thought was completely private and only for the five of them. Nevaeh's names for their fellow students and teachers and the in-jokes Aaliyah shared seemed special and a unique part of what made them all friends.

Sure, Rylee had known she wasn't in the inner-*inner* circle—that space was reserved for Nevaeh alone, who had known Aaliyah since she was born. Rylee, Rosario, and Cherise kind of took turns being the one Aaliyah called when she needed something. Sometimes it *had* felt a little lonely when it wasn't Rylee's "turn" to be special to Aaliyah or when Nevaeh gave off strong *back-off* vibes when Rylee had laughed too loudly at something Rosario said or seemed to be having too much fun with Aaliyah. But, as long as she'd been included, Rylee had been able to shove down the worrying little voice in her head that said that the five of them weren't the nicest people. As long as she'd been on the inside, it hadn't mattered that much. Rylee knew better than to be snide and rude like that—she wasn't mean or anything really. But when it was just Aaliyah being funny . . . it hadn't mattered that much.

Rylee shifted uncomfortably, and one of the girls looked over at her.

When she whispered to her friend the next time, Rylee was positive it was about her. Rolling her eyes at their nonsense, she stood and put down her book on a convenient table. It was definitely past time to get out of there. She'd just pop into the bathroom and walk home the long way, so she could stop by the weird little tool store on Forsythia Street that Daddy Warren liked and buy a bag of kettle chips.

When Rylee came out of the bathroom stall, though, her happy plan evaporated. Cherise, wearing her gray "cherry bomb" hoodie with the pair of eight-ball cherries on the chest, was leaning against the wall by the sinks, tightening her ponytail.

"Girl, I *thought* it was you," Cherise said, straightening. "I remember when you said you were going to get those blue extensions, and you did. They're super cute."

The first thing Rylee was going to do when she got home was take out those extensions.

Jeez. Her heart squeezed so hard that she was sure it had missed a few beats. Rylee couldn't unfreeze her face enough to open her mouth, and even if she could have, she wasn't sure she knew what she was supposed to say. Cherise was just—smiling at her, talking, like nothing had ever happened, like she hadn't done anything wrong. Maybe she thought she hadn't—it's not like it was against school rules to be mean to someone at Nevaeh Green's house.

Rylee forced herself to move.

She took a breath and stepped toward the line of sinks farthest away from Cherise, waving her hands under the sensor for the soap. The automatic dispenser delivered a blue-tinged pile of foam into Rylee's hands, and she scrubbed, internally reciting two verses of "Twinkle, Twinkle, Little Star" twice over while she washed. The twenty seconds to prevent viruses passed, then twenty more.

When the blazing sun is gone, when he nothing shines upon . . .

Rylee couldn't seem to stop moving her hands, scrubbing between her fingers, ringing around her wrist and thumb. Cherise wasn't leaving, and she wasn't going into a stall, either. Had Aaliyah *sent* her to talk to Rylee? Did anyone else know she was there, at the library? If Cherise was there, where was everyone else?

Then you show your little light, twinkle, twinkle, all the night . . .

Cherise's smile wavered, then became an awkward grimace. "So . . . I guess you're still mad about last year," she stated, as if Nevaeh's party in May had been last Christmas instead of only three months ago. "It . . . it wasn't supposed to be like, a big Thing. It was just . . ." Cherise took a breath as the words came faster. "Well, you know, Aaliyah said you stuffed your top at the party, because Jackson kind of looked at you when he saw you by the pool, and Nevaeh said she'd just grab your stuff and check your bra size, only it was just some random number, and we couldn't tell anything from that, so Aaliyah said we could just take your clothes and . . . see if you did . . ." Cherise trailed off as Rylee waved her hands under the water. It gushed out strongly enough that Rylee wouldn't have heard if Cherise had kept on talking.

At least now she wasn't scared or numb anymore. Now Rylee felt like she'd had some kind of chili peppers shoved directly into her chest. If she said anything now, her words might come out like she was breathing fire.

It was a total *lie*. Aaliyah hadn't wanted to know anything, and Nevaeh hadn't gone into her bag just to "check" something. Aaliyah didn't just dig for information; she demanded it. If she'd really wanted to know Rylee's size, she would have asked for it. She would have had Rylee whisper it into her ear, then she would have shouted it out by the side of the pool, while Nevaeh laughed hysterically. That's how Aaliyah rolled—right over people, smash and grab, letting them in on the joke while she was laughing at them.

Even Cherise didn't believe what she was saying, and by the way she suddenly looked down to examine her cute black boots, Rylee could tell. Jackson had "kind of" looked at her, and Aaliyah and Nevaeh had decided to humiliate her—to get back at her when it hadn't even been her fault.

Rylee took another deep breath and turned toward the paper towel dispenser. She could have used the blower to dry her hands, but she wanted to give Cherise a chance to say the two important words she hadn't yet. Rylee pulled a scratchy brown paper from the dispenser and blotted the water from her hands, raising narrowed eyes to her former friend's.

But just as Cherise opened her mouth, a mother hustled a small child into the bathroom, chanting, "Hurry-hurry-hurry!" By the time Rylee had turned back from throwing her paper towel away, the door was closing, and Cherise was—gone.

The fire in Rylee's chest *roared*, flames rising to

make her face burn and her eyes water.

That was . . . *it*? No "I'm sorry"? No "I wish you still hung out with us"? No "That was kind of mean, and I know we owe you an apology"? Cherise was going to talk about her extensions, and that was all?

Shaking, Rylee exited the bathroom and hurried through the library. Other than the good soup she'd had at the café, the day had been a waste. She wished she hadn't even gotten out of bed.

9

Wrong Story

Later that day, Rylee headed downstairs to the hallway outside her grandparents' bedroom, to Geema's "hair wardrobe." Originally, the tall wooden cabinet with the mirrored double doors had been in the back of Geema's real closet. She'd rearranged things and added a new storage system for her "ninety-five pairs of shoes," as Daddy Warren numbered them (Rylee had counted only thirty-four, plus Geema's two pairs of furry slipper-boots), so the shelves full of wig stands and zippered plastic envelopes full of hair extensions had a new home.

As long as she was careful and left everything as she'd found it (no knots, no tangles), Geema had never minded Rylee playing with her wigs. When she came down the hall that evening and found Rylee clipping in some long, silver extensions in place of her blue ones, her grandmother smiled.

"Well, that's a . . . look," Geema chuckled, stepping around Rylee and continuing to her bedroom. The scent of her perfume floated through the hall. "I think it's a little early for you to be going gray, though."

"No, it's the style now," Rylee disagreed, but she started taking out the extensions and laying them back into their container anyway. "Did you and Ms. Grace have a nice time at your play?"

Geema made a positive sound. "You should have come. I loved the costumes. I didn't like the man they had playing the villain, though. He looked way too cute to be a bad guy."

Rylee had finished putting things away by the time Geema changed into a pair of pink sweats with leopard-print capital letters spelling the word "BLESSED" across the sweatshirt. Her matching leopard-print slippers slapped her heels as she went down the hall to the kitchen, sweeping Rylee up in a side hug as she went. "Well, what are you up to this afternoon?"

Rylee made a face. "Nothing. I've been doing homework all day. Hey—Geema, do you think you and

Daddy Warren would want to help me with something?"

Geema paused while digging through the cabinets for her tea and fixed Rylee with a sharp look. "Help you *how*, missy? You're working on that 'scientific journalism,' but my days of doing homework are long over."

"I just meant I need you to answer some questions for me. Questions about friendship," Rylee said, trying not to smile. Geema always made a point of letting Rylee and Axel know they needed to find Daddy Warren or Mom whenever they needed homework help.

Geema visibly relaxed. "Oh. Friendship? That sounds interesting."

"Actually, I might want to ask more than you and Ms. Grace," Rylee said slowly as the idea gelled. "We were thinking of asking a bunch of people—do you think any of your other friends would do a questionnaire if it was only, like, five or six questions?"

Geema set her blue kettle on the smooth glass surface of the electric stove and turned it on. "I'm sure some of them wouldn't mind helping you out, but first, why don't you sit down and talk to me about what you're trying to do?"

Rylee pulled out a chair at the kitchen table and

dropped onto it, rubbing her forehead. She wasn't sure how much to say. "So . . . I already told you about my journalism elective," she began, and Geema leaned against the counter, nodding.

"Well, the project is about how most junior high friendships *end*, and at first, we were going to just stick to that part of the question, but I guess I just started thinking . . . I mean, you and Ms. Grace have known each other since elementary. Daddy Warren was friends with you in high school. I know people are different today, but I just don't get . . . how come people from back in the day were better at being friends? I thought, if I could figure *that* out, then I could add that to the paper, you know? Like, 'Five ways to have an old-school friendship' or something."

Geema's face went through a series of expressions—a little blink, confusion, and then she laughed. "I don't think my friendships are something easy to write down in five steps," she said with another chuckle. "In Daddy Warren's case it was more like, 'Putting up with that annoying boy for four years until he kind of grew on me.'"

Rylee rolled her eyes. She knew all about how Daddy Warren had been one of the boys Geema had baked cookies for every single day in ninth grade home ec class—it didn't seem like he'd annoyed her all *that* much.

"And as for Ms. Grace—well, I told you we never let little things come in between us."

Rylee frowned slightly. "I don't even know what that means."

Geema pressed her lips to the side in thought, studying the ceiling for a moment before looking back at Rylee. "Well, now, I can explain, but . . . you have to understand that I didn't understand it, either, when I was your age, not *entirely*."

"You . . . didn't?" Rylee asked, brows raised. Usually, Geema told stories about how she'd been a good friend and an excellent student and an obedient child who never talked back, and never, *ever* rolled her eyes when she'd been Rylee's age. "What do you mean, 'explain'?"

"Well." Geema turned as the kettle began to sing and poured hot water into a small glass teapot with a matching cup. "You want some tea, Ry? I have a nice licorice tea, or there's a bag of that chamomile left. I'm making a pot of Lapsang souchong. We have some gingersnaps, too."

"I'd like some gingersnaps, but no tea, please," said Rylee, who thought Geema's Lapsang tea smelled like old campfires and tasted like burnt barbecue. "So, you let a little thing get between you and Ms. Grace when you were young?" she pried. It seemed like Geema was stalling.

"A little bit, a little bit," Geema said reflectively, setting a plate of cookies in front of Rylee and carefully placing the small teapot on a metal trivet. She settled into the cushioned kitchen chair. "As it happened, in middle school, Ms. Grace and I auditioned for a new version of *The Nutcracker* for our winter talent show."

"That sounds fun," Rylee said, trying to imagine Geema exchanging fuzzy leopard-print mules for ballet shoes. "But . . . I guess it wasn't?"

"It was fun—at first," Geema said, settling back in her seat. "When I was your age, there were a lot of movies about dancing, a lot of TV shows about kids in arts schools who were going to make it big in New York. Our school hired a drama teacher who also taught dance, and every girl in our junior high tried out for the winter show. It was going to be fun and different, and everyone wanted a part. Of course, they couldn't take everyone."

Rylee looked at her tall, queenly looking grandmother, and thought of Ms. Grace, who was short and curvy, with short legs. *Oh.*

"Ms. Grace didn't get to dance in *The Nutcracker*, did she?" Rylee realized.

Geema cackled. "Oh, Gracie was a shoo-in. *I* was the one who was too tall and had too-long arms. Every time I turned, I whacked into the girl next to me. I couldn't follow directions to save my life and kept turning left while everyone else turned right." Geema shook her head. "The dance teacher was gentle, but she told me it might be better if I worked on costumes or backdrops with the other students who didn't have 'the gift of dance.'"

"Ooh, burn." Rylee made a face. Even if the teacher had meant to be kind, that was *embarrassing*.

Geema smiled. "But Grace had more elegance in her pinky finger than I had in my whole body—she could turn and twirl and follow all that crazy choreography like she was born to do it. They gave the sixth and seventh graders the smallest parts, since we were the youngest, but instead of being a mouse or a soldier, Grace got to be part of the actual ballet dancers. She was the only sixth grader who got picked to dance with the eighth graders. I was so humiliated. I stomped off that stage so mad, I could spit."

Rylee's eyes widened. "Geema!"

"I know, right?" Geema said, scrunching up her face. "And wouldn't it have been dumb if I'd been picked to be in *The Nutcracker* and I couldn't even dance? But I wasn't hearing from common sense right then. I was in my feelings, and I figured since I didn't get picked, Grace shouldn't agree to take a part, either. She . . . disagreed. Pretty loudly, actually."

Rylee blinked. "So, what did you do?"

Geema shrugged. "Fought about it the whole two months of rehearsals. Trash-talked Grace every chance I got. Tagged her locker with nail polish and almost got suspended."

"You tagged her— Geema, *what*!?" Rylee gasped. "That's messed up!" This wasn't a "little bit" like Geema had said. This was *major*! "Then what happened?" Rylee blurted.

"We both got called to the principal's office. Mrs. Watkins told us that every friendship comes to a place where the friends have to decide what's more important—the other person, or the argument." Geema paused and sipped her tea.

"And I guess you both decided each other was more important," Rylee said, settling back in the kitchen chair, because that was obviously the way the story was supposed to go. This was Geema and Ms. Grace, after all, the besties who'd been BFFs since Moses was a tiny baby.

"Of course we did," Geema said warmly, setting down her cup. "But not that day. That day we decided not to speak to each other for the rest of sixth grade."

Rylee sat back, shocked. *"What!?"*

Leaning gloomily against the door of her bedroom, Rylee threaded narrow strips of paper into the quilling tool Mom had found her at the craft store and tightly twisted the paper into quills. This questionnaire was—well, it wasn't good. Geema's story had given her a place to start, but that was the problem—it was just a story. It wasn't facts, or reasoning, or something that could fit into a scientific survey . . . not to mention that she could not *believe* that Geema had been low-key lying to her about her perfect friendship with Ms. Grace all this time. *Ugh!*

Pulling another strip of paper from her box, Rylee once again read over the page-long list of questions she had created. It was . . . terrible. The questions were either too nosy or too dumb. They were boring and didn't sound science-y enough.

THE SEGREST FRIENDSHIP SURVEY

What makes a best friend? They (pick one):

    a. Always tell the truth, even if it hurts

    b. Let you copy homework

    c. Make you want to be better

    d. Have your same sense of humor

    e. Cheer for you even when they're on the other team

    f. Know personal deets about your family

    g. Don't have to worry about paying you back when they borrow

    h. Tell you all their secret crushes

    i. Hate the people you hate

    j. Have all the same interests as you

    k. None of the above (fill in your own answer)

What is the most important quality a friend should have? They (pick one):

    a. Always have your back, even if you might be wrong

    b. Never criticize and always make you feel good about everything you do

    c. Never tease/laugh at you

   d. Always listen to the whole story before they react

How do you fix friendship problems? Do you:
   a. Stop talking / ignore a problem till it goes away
   b. Decide whose fault it is and confront them
   c. Tell the person how you feel and what you think
   d. Apologize for everything, even if it's not your fault
   e. Decide it's not worth fixing it if you're fighting

The whole list was all wrong.

The friendship surveys online weren't like this. They sounded like the types of things Ms. Johnston wanted in the school paper—like something fun to do when you were at someone's house after school and you were bored. Rylee's questions sounded like a test for a class she wasn't sure she'd pass.

And Geema! Rylee dropped the last spiral of paper and growled a little under her breath. Geema was supposed to be her secret weapon! Geema was where she *thought* she was going to figure out her whole project.

She'd acted like she had the perfect friendship with Ms. Grace for eleventy-billion years, and *now* was when she decided to tell Rylee that wasn't really true!?

Geema had seemed a little startled when she'd seen the expression on Rylee's face.

"But—I—you said you didn't let little things come between you!"

"Well, we didn't, as I said, not forever," Geema assured her, picking up her teacup again. "It took some doing, but since we were working each other's nerves showing up in the same places, doing all the same things, we decided to call a truce and be polite, at least. Until the next holiday show, when we had to sing a duet." Geema smiled at the memory.

Ugh. And probably after another argument, they'd found the perfect song that reminded them of friendship, and then they were the best singers in the holiday show, and once again became the most perfect best friends, like a Disney movie with singing mice. Rylee hadn't even asked to hear the end of that story. All she knew was that wouldn't, *couldn't* be the ending to her story. The thought of *ever* being best friends again with Aaliyah and Nevaeh made her stomach curdle.

Frustrated, she stabbed another strip of paper into the narrow slot on the quilling tool. When the paper crumpled, she had to do it again, more carefully, and used her irritation to twist an especially tight quill.

Her story wasn't the same, of course. Geema and Ms. Grace had just been best friends with each other. Rylee had been friends with Aaliyah *and* Nevaeh, *and* Cherise *and* Rosario, but it hadn't mattered. When Aaliyah stopped being friendly, *none* of the girls had acted friendly with Rylee anymore.

Rylee twisted another strip of paper into a tight circle. She hated to admit DeNia was right about anything, but news writing *was* turning out to be hard, harder than it looked. What made this science news? How much of this news was science?

Rylee rubbed her face and slumped in her chair, pressing her head to the padded headrest.

Fact: Rylee needed help. *Badly.* She wasn't comfortable pretending to be a scientist, thinking up questions to ask and getting anonymous answers from people she didn't know. She wanted to sit down and ask questions of her fellow classmates, hear their stories, and try to figure out what everything meant. This survey wasn't going to work like this—not without DeNia's help, and Rylee wasn't about to call her. Not now. She *had* to do this by herself, even if it was just to prove that she could.

10

Crossroads and Questions

As the sun went down, Rylee found she was fighting end-of-weekend blues. She stared out the window, poked through her closet, and sighed a lot.

From across the hall, Rylee heard Axel laughing his dorky snort-laugh, and rolled her eyes. Her brother was playing that stupid 100 Wizards game with his friends again. No matter how dumb he sounded when he was playing—now he was cackling and yelling something about ninth-level monsters—at least he actually had *friends*, since none of them had suddenly ditched him for being annoying. Come to think of it, though, *all* of Axel's friends were annoying.

When they got together, the amount of thumping

and rattling that shook the room as they wrestled and laughed and threw things at each other was ridiculous. Rylee tried to remember if she'd been as goofy when she was eleven. When she'd been in the sixth grade, she'd been mostly trying to talk Mom into letting her walk downtown with friends to get fries after school and experimenting with Geema's nail glue and fake nails (she'd stopped after an incident with glue, her two middle fingers, and the top of Geema's vanity). She'd hung out with a lot of different girls, like Rena and Devon. Rena had moved away that year, the same year Nevaeh had come to Segrest, but Devon was . . . wasn't Devon still at Segrest?

Rylee frowned thoughtfully. She'd seen her around last year a bit, but . . . how had she lost track of someone she'd hung out with so much? When had Aaliyah's friends taken the place of hers?

That . . . sounded like a good question, actually. She should write that down for the article, probably.

Rylee grabbed her phone and opened the Notes 2 Self app.

Question: When do new friends take the place of old ones?

Hypothesis: People make new friends as often as

people change = all the time

Prediction: Most junior high students will have different friends by the end of the school year.

Experiment: Check DeNia's study. Is there a new one? Check dates.

Analysis: Read student surveys and compare how and why people make new friends. Is it true only at Segrest School, or in the world?

The world? *Ugh.* That made zero sense. Nothing was true all over the world. Nobody needed a hypothesis when she was *proof* that you could start junior high with one set of friends, and then not have them anymore. Rylee felt like she'd been working on this pointless survey all weekend, and it was only getting worse.

Axel banged across the hall into the bathroom next door to Rylee's room, and she heard him humming the theme to his video game as the toilet flushed and the sink ran.

Rylee rolled to her feet. This wasn't the kind of question that DeNia would ask—maybe asking her brother wasn't science-y enough, but Ms. Johnston would probably think her brother was good source material for one of the three pieces she needed to turn in, at least.

"Axel," she called, stepping into the hall.

"What?" Axel said defensively, opening the bathroom door and scuttling back to the safety of his doorway. "The seat is down already."

"Good for you," Rylee said, making a disgusted face. "Hey—do you remember the name of your first friend?"

Axel's face wrinkled. "What? Why?"

"Research," Rylee said, waving an impatient hand. "Answer the question."

"Um . . . I met Blake in kindergarten," her brother said, naming his best friend. "I don't remember anyone else."

"Do you guys ever fight?"

Axel slumped against the doorjamb like a puppet with its strings cut. "Ry*lee*."

"What? What's wrong with asking that?"

"No quiero hablar." Axel used his sixth-grade Spanish lessons, as if English wasn't getting through to her. "I'm in the middle of a game."

Rylee bit back a sigh. A good journalist knew when to back off and let her source take a breath. "Fine— if you don't want to talk right this second, will you promise to answer some questions for me another time? It's for a class."

"Are you paying?" Axel looked skeptical.

Rylee debated with herself for a moment. Axel already owed her a small favor, but she wanted to hold that for something more important. "Maybe. What do you want?"

Her brother paused. "Um . . . would you put the trash out for me tomorrow night?"

Bagging the kitchen trash and dragging the cans for garbage, food waste, and recycling out to the curb wasn't hard—just kind of annoying, and the cobwebs on the cans were gross, but Rylee could wear a pair of Geema's rubber gloves. She was getting Axel for cheap.

"Okay, but will you answer all the questions? Even the weird ones?"

Axel stuck out a fist. Rylee tapped it, then bumped knuckles and wriggled her thumbs in the secret handshake Axel had come up with when he was seven. "Deal," they said in unison.

"Should I worry that you two are merging your wonder-twin powers?" Mom asked, padding down the hallway to the stairs, carrying an empty mug.

"What?" Sometimes her mother said the weirdest things. "Actually, Mom . . . do you have time to answer a couple of questions?"

"I guess?" Mom said, looking back over her shoulder. "Is this about your paper-quill project in advisory again?"

"Not this time," Rylee said. "It's for my journalism elective."

"Oh—interesting. Give me a minute," Mom said, going downstairs.

Eagerly, Rylee returned to her room to grab her laptop, meeting her mother on her way back to her bedroom. Rylee sat in her usual spot on the floor as her mother went into the closet to pull out a foam rubber mat. Mom set a basket full of nail polish on the rolled-out mat and pulled off her socks.

"So, this is for your elective project. How's that going, anyway?"

"It's fine," Rylee said, then added, "Kind of. I'm just in the beginning stage, but I have some questions I want to ask everyone at school. If they seem . . . weird or too personal, can you tell me?"

"Sure," Mom said. She sat down, shaking the bottle of nail polish she'd selected. "I'm ready."

Rylee's eyes flew to the pearly white nail polish, and she shook her head, once again flabbergasted at the memory of the wise, classy Geema that she knew, going full Spite Sister on a locker with a tiny flat brush.

Suddenly, Rylee knew what she wanted to ask. "Mom," she said eagerly, "Question One."

You and your closest friend audition for a show. Your friend gets in. You get asked to make costumes and paint scenery with the other people who can't dance, sing, or act. Do you:
  a. Pick up a brush, even though your painting stinks
  b. Ask your friend to bow out, and join an activity you can do together
  c. Ignore the show—avoid rehearsals and performances to keep the peace
  d. Tell your friend to quit, and trash-talk her when she won't

"Wow," Rylee's mother laughed. "Those are . . . that's a good question. Um . . . I think I choose option *B*," she continued. "I can't sew, and I don't know if I'd be very good at the whole backdrop thing. We could find something else to do together."

"Huh. Okay, *B*," Rylee said, making an imaginary mark in the air. She'd kind of thought Mom would have just kept quiet and avoided everything, but that was maybe more like what *Rylee* would have done herself. Mom had *liked* the question, though, so these were probably the *kinds* of questions that she could ask on her official survey.

Rylee made sure her expression didn't give anything away as she asked the next question. "Right. Question Two."

You and a friend are working on a class project. Your friend sometimes works on the project by herself, without telling you first. When you try to add a new part to the project, your friend complains that you're not doing it right. Do you:

    a. Erase your part and do the project exactly like your friend wants you to

    b. Tell your friend that you have good ideas, too, and make her listen

    c. Do separate projects so you both can work by yourselves

    d. Decide to just go with it, since your friend will get you both a good grade

"Answers *A* and *D* might be a little too much alike," her mother gave her critique. "Maybe you can try adding more people to the group project so there's more people to work on all the parts? And then both you and your friend get what you want."

"Hmm! Interesting," Rylee said, trying to imagine adding even more people to her and DeNia's project. It would be a disaster.

"Anyway, I'd definitely pick C," Mom added, finishing her left pinkie toe. "If she wants to do the project that much, she can do the whole thing." She looked up at Rylee, who was smiling. "I'm doing okay, right? I mean, these don't have right answers? They're just questions?"

"Oh, there's no right answer," Rylee said, grinning. "I just thought this one was funny, that's all. Ready?" Her mother nodded. "Ready. Hit me."

You run into an ex-friend at Juice Jungle. Even though they know why you're not hanging with the group anymore, they talk to you like nothing happened, and they don't apologize for what they did. Do you:

    a. Stand in line for your Simba Smoothie like they don't exist

    b. Pretend like you meet for smoothies every Sunday and act normal

    c. Drag them to the parking lot to throw down and hash it out

    d. Be civil, say hi, and accept that friendship
        fade happens and it's okay

"Ugh, *A*," Mom said immediately. Then she sighed. "No, I'm lying. *D*. I'm supposed to choose *D*."

"There's not one you're supposed to choose," Rylee insisted, resting her laptop on her knees. "I promise, I just made these up because I think they're good questions. People . . . should know how to act when something like this happens. People should understand *what to do*." Rylee wished again that she had even known that there *was* something to do, other than put up with it.

"School would certainly have been easier if someone had written a book or something," Mom muttered, closing the polish. "How many more of these are there? I was going to watch a show with Geema."

"Um, just a couple, but they might need rewriting," Rylee said, looking at her laptop again. There was nothing written there at all, but she kept staring at the blank square where words would be typed.

"You're at a party when four of your best friends . . . um, *prank you when you're changing out of your swimsuit by stealing your dry clothes, hiding in a closet, and,* um . . . *laughing. You . . .* uh, you . . ."

Rylee cleared her throat, just then realizing that her mother was sitting frozen, the nail polish clutched in her hand.

"Um . . . I think I might need to work on this one a little bit. It's kind of too long."

"Hold up," her mother said, her eyes narrowing. "*Rylee*. Is this what hap—?"

"Just a sec, I have one last question!" Rylee interrupted. "Okay, so—"

You go back-to-school shopping, and you see a top you like. You're excited, because you know someone who works at the store and can get it with their employee discount. You wear it the first day of school, but your friend says you can't wear it again because they bought a shirt exactly like it. Do you:

    a. Tell your friend they can't always get their own way, and wear it proudly

    b. Suggest a friend day and promise to only wear the shirts together

    c. Return the shirt to the store and get new shoes—it's not worth the drama

    d. Put the shirt away until next year—your friend will like something else by then

There was a pause, then her mother said firmly, "A, it's definitely A. It's my shirt, and they can just *deal* with it if they don't like it. Now, Ry," she added, rushing out the words, "we need to walk back to that last question . . ."

Rylee shifted uncomfortably. "I told you, they're not done, Mom," she said quickly, closing the cover on her laptop. Mom didn't need to know that some of the questions were from her real-life experiences.

Her mother ignored this. "You mentioned Nevaeh's pool party the other day. Is the previous question what happened with Ms. Grace's granddaughter? Are she and Nevaeh bullying you at school? You don't have to tell me anything—but you can." Her mother was sitting forward, her hands braced against the floor beside her, as if she was just holding herself back from leaping up to tackle something.

"Mama, nobody's bullying me," Rylee said, trying to laugh it off, even though her chest felt tight. "Bullying" was a word that meant somebody was being hassled and made afraid over and over again, not a word that had anything to do with her. Aaliyah hadn't *bullied* her. She and Nevaeh had just been being mean, like they sometimes were, and some people had gone along with it, that was all. And now Mom was upset. Rylee knew she shouldn't have said anything. She'd only wanted to know if Mom thought she'd done the right thing, but—

"Nobody?" Her mother's eyes narrowed. "Are you sure? Rylee . . . I'm happy to take some time off of work and talk to parents if I need to," she said, her expression fierce. "If someone is bullying *my* daughter, we will *fix it*. We do not sit around and pretend it's all good in this house."

"Mom, nobody's bothering me at school." Rylee carefully tiptoed around the truth—it hadn't happened *at* school, after all. She *could* tell Mom what happened—at least Ms. Grace and Geema would be upset—but she wasn't six and crying about someone pushing her down on the playground. It was *way* past time for Mom to be fighting her battles. "And—I know I can talk to you, Mom. I appreciate you and Geema and Daddy Warren . . . a lot. If something happens at school, I'll let you know. I just . . . I don't want to make a big deal out of anything. I just need to do this survey thing, and forget about it, okay?"

Mom bit her bottom lip and studied Rylee, her shoulders lowering with the force of her gusty sigh. "Okay," she said slowly. "I hear you. You're the leader on this, so if you don't want to make a big deal about how those girls treated you, we won't. But, Rylee—I don't want you lugging worries around all by yourself. It's my job to help you, to talk to you, and to listen. If you don't want me, we can find someone else for you to talk to—a therapist, a teacher at school, someone. All of us have been there—all of us have had bad friendships before, even Geema."

At that, Rylee smiled faintly. This was familiar territory. "I know."

"Well . . . good," her mother said, tapping her nail polish bottle against her palm. "If you've got more questions for me—about anything at all—just ask, all right? Let someone help you, Rylee Rae. Life is hard enough. Nobody said you've got to figure it out all by yourself."

"I know, Mom," Rylee said again. She let her mother give her a full-body squeeze, hugging until her ribs felt a little bit like they were bending where there weren't any hinges.

"Ow!" she complained and escaped. But she felt her mother's hug the whole rest of the night.

11

Blast from the Past

Her mother was so glad Rylee asked her for help with something that she'd braided the silver-gray extensions into Rylee's hair the next morning without even making a comment about the color. Rylee loved the striking contrast of dark and light cornrows that snaked from either side of her middle part and lay thick and smooth against her shoulders. They looked even cooler with her white T-shirt dress, sleeveless denim jacket, and black-and-white low-top canvas shoes. If Mom hadn't been still braiding her hair at the last second, Geema would have made her do another runway strut.

"Monday had better get out of your way!" Geema

crowed as Rylee crunched through her bowl of cereal. "My girl is here to slay, *all* day."

"Thank you very much," Rylee said, drawling a little as she channeled her favorite cartoon voice. She leaned over her grandmother and gave her a hug. "Oh, um, Geema. Will you talk to Ms. Grace today, and ask if she has time for my interview questions?"

Geema gave her a thumbs-up and swallowed the last swig of her coffee. "I'm on it. That's all taken care of, sweetheart."

Mom leaned over Rylee's shoulder as she tucked in a hairpin. "Are you asking her the same questions you asked me last night?"

"Yes—but I also need some quotes for the article. I'm asking Axel and Geema, so we can get, like, an idea about friendship from different ages. Geema's asking Ms. Grace to help, and I might ask Daddy Warren, too."

"*Hmm,*" her mother had said. "This should be interesting."

Even though her hair got lots of compliments—and a side-eyed up-and-down examination of her entire look from Cherise in the hallway—Rylee discovered she was nervous walking into homeroom on Monday morning. DeNia hadn't just texted; the previous night she'd called Rylee, but, still a little mad at how DeNia had blown off her project idea, Rylee had accidentally-on-purpose turned off her ringer.

At first, it seemed like it just served DeNia right—Rylee had been too tired to deal with friend drama, especially after Mom had lurked around all evening, trying to make sure she wasn't somehow itching to talk and just hadn't been able to walk all the way down the hall toward her mother's bedroom. Even though she *had* been kind of busy, Rylee had made enough "just saying hey" calls to friends before to know it wasn't a good feeling to not have them returned. DeNia hadn't left a message, and as Rylee walked down the aisle toward her homeroom seat, she wished she'd just called DeNia back and gotten whatever drama was going to happen between them over with before school.

As Rylee sat in her usual seat, DeNia stayed head down, her narrow back in the forest-green T-shirt hunched like a small hill. Her backpack was, for once, between her feet instead of gaping open, spilling her business into the aisle. DeNia was writing quickly in a small, spiral-bound blank book.

"Hey," Rylee said hesitantly.

"Just a sec," DeNia mumbled, scrawling out a last

word. She exhaled slowly as she scanned the page, then closed the notebook and thrust it toward Rylee. "Okay. Since we didn't get to talk last night, I have some notes."

"Notes." Rylee stared down at the wire-bound pad of paper. This reminded her a lot of the morning when DeNia had given her a stack of research, and wasn't *that* a tiny bit ominous? "Soooo, did you *write* these? Or is this more research?"

DeNia frowned, looking confused. "It's just some stuff I wrote."

Rylee shook her head, also confused. "But, I'm right here. Wouldn't it be easier to just . . . tell me what you want to say? You could have even left me a voice mail last night."

DeNia shrugged. "I could have, but my dad always says to write stuff down 'cause people don't listen."

"I listen," Rylee protested, then rolled her eyes at herself. Hadn't she learned before there wasn't any point in arguing with DeNia over anything? And she hadn't been all that willing to listen last night, had she? "Never mind. Thanks, DeNia." Rylee shoved the paper into her backpack and settled into her seat to watch the morning announcements. She'd read the notes and worry about what DeNia wanted later.

As the student reporter droned on about new junior high clubs, Rylee realized that if something like this had happened with Aaliyah or Nevaeh, she would have had a stomachache right then. She would have taken any sign her friends were mad at her as something she deserved and would have been stupidly relieved when whatever drama blew over.

Somehow, it didn't hit the same way with DeNia. Rylee was a little let down that DeNia had been salty at the café, and she was weirded out by the girl's paper obsession (how many notebooks did a person *need*?), but otherwise, even though neither of them seemed to be feeling entirely friendly yet, Rylee was surprised to realize that she wasn't . . . worried about it. She'd usually felt either upset or anxious being friends with the Spite Sisters, feelings that had lasted for so long that their absence was . . . weird. Rylee imagined herself writing a survey question about it, and snickered:

Your new friend turns out to be super crabby for some reason and blows off your ideas when you meet. The next time she sees you, she acts like everything is cool. Do you:

    a. Let it go—that happened Sunday, and it's a new day now

b. Worry about how you messed up and tell your new friend you're sorry

c. Decide if your friend isn't mad, then you don't have to be, either

d. Wait for your new friend to apologize—or else you're not friends anymore

When the announcements finished, DeNia leaned across the aisle and spoke in a rushed undertone.

"Okay—since you haven't read the notes yet, I'll give you the recap. You have good ideas, and I have good ideas, and we can put them together to make something great." DeNia nodded, as if it was all settled. "I *did* write up another project pitch for Ms. Johnston—I mean, we *can* turn in more than our three pieces—but I still think a collaborative article could work. So, I put down some of my ideas in there." She jerked her chin, indicating the spiral notebook.

"DeNia—" Rylee began.

DeNia shifted in her seat, looking away. "Unless you don't want to work with me. Which I understand completely, if you're still mad, but—"

"I'm not mad," Rylee said quickly, "but, DeNia, come on. The problem we had before is that we're not interested in the same things. Plus, you're good at the science, and I'm good"—Rylee shrugged—"at talking to people, maybe? I read some of the articles you got me, and they're interesting and all, but I don't know how they're about people at Segrest right now. I want to ask questions and dig into why people here do stuff and write about that. That's not really science, I don't think, so—"

"Yes, it is," DeNia broke in quickly. "It's studying people, sociology and psychology, and talking is a completely legit social science. You can do interviewing and surveying, and I'll look at articles and statistics. We'll put it all together, and it'll be even better." DeNia hefted her backpack as people stood to go to their next classes. "Just . . . read my notes. I'll talk to you at advisory?"

"Okay, sure," Rylee said, grabbing her own bag. So, talking to people was science . . . ? And, DeNia wanted to keep working together. That was probably good. It meant she might actually manage to turn in at least one article and get a decent grade. Rylee exhaled a relieved breath and stepped into the chaos of the hallway.

Rylee had just slid the notebook from beneath her geometry book during a pause in another of Mr.

Pfister's lightning-fast chapter reviews when some-one eased open the heavy classroom door and stepped inside. Distracted, Rylee glanced up—then did a double take.

She was taller than she'd been in sixth grade—she'd been pretty much queen of the krill back then, so that was good—but her thick, dark hair, long-lashed brown eyes, and sharp-chinned face were still the same. The girl's quick look swept the room before she handed her pass to Mr. Pfister.

"Devon Eastman, great. Why don't you have a seat?" the geometry teacher said, reaching for a sheet of paper and giving her some other instructions Rylee paid no attention to.

She couldn't help leaning forward to stare as Devon sat down a couple of rows away. Same oversize comic book T-shirts—though this was pretty clearly from the latest *Wonder Woman* movie, so it was new. Same camouflage pants and battered high-tops. Same mannerisms—the dense curls muscling free of her ponytail holder were tucked automatically behind her ears, just like always. Sixth-grade Devon had hated math, though, so her joining a section of Geometry II was a major change. The Devon that Rylee remembered would have done her best to stay in seventh-grade foundational math until the end of time.

Rylee snuck another look as Mr. Pfister started talking again. She had a sudden memory of Devon in a pair of these gray-and-black urban camo pants she'd practically lived in, and Aaliyah teasing her one day.

"So, Devon . . . are you supposed to be invisible? Like, are we not supposed to see you today?"

Rylee, who had never understood Devon's obsession with wearing dull colors and random patterns, had laughed. Devon hadn't.

Rylee rolled her mechanical pencil between her fingers as she remembered her and Devon's kind-of argument, with Rylee swearing she hadn't been laughing *at* Devon, and Devon ranting that people who tried to dictate what other people wore were total snotwaffles. Rylee had agreed, of course, but then Devon had doubled down on wearing camouflage—and Rylee had brought it up again.

"It's not even like you hunt, or you're a soldier or something," Rylee had said, leaning against the wall as they waited their turn for a handball court. "You could pull off something really cute, like . . . Rena's shorts," Rylee said, gesturing at the girl currently trouncing her opponent. "Or, the denim ones Aaliyah has, with the lace peeking out. Don't you think they're cute?"

"I told you, I don't like shorts," Devon had grumped, swiping her thick bangs out of her eyes. "Rena says my legs are too fuzzy, but I don't want to start shaving or I can't ever quit. Why does anyone care so much what I wear? You sound just like my mom." Devon had pitched her voice high and nasally. "'Devon, honey, don't you want to look more like a girl?'"

"Calm down, Devon, sheesh! I don't care what you wear," Rylee had said, throwing up her hands. "I just think Aaliyah's shorts are cute, that's it."

But that hadn't been the end of it, not quite. Rylee had liked Aaliyah's shorts so well that she'd carefully cut up an old, stained doily Geema had used under a plant in the living room and sewed it with slightly crooked stitches onto the bottom of her own cut-off denims.

"Those are cuuuute!" Aaliyah had said when Rylee had gotten to school.

"Thanks!" Rylee had beamed. "They took, like, for-ever, but I like them."

"You did them yourself? You can *sew?*" Aaliyah's voice dropped to a whisper as Mrs. Goins started taking attendance. "Hey, sit with me at lunch and tell me how you did it."

Rylee had smiled so widely for the rest of that day

that her face had hurt by the time she'd gone home. It wasn't a big deal for Rena, the other member of their friend trio, to eat with her tumbling team friends or, more accurately, go outside and do cartwheels through lunch instead of eating. But Devon and Rylee always sat together, and always at the same table, and they always brought lunch from home on Breakfast for Lunch days in the cafeteria—mostly so they could share the homemade breakfast burritos Devon's mother made. They'd been sitting together for so long that Rylee had automatically invited Devon to sit with her and Aaliyah. And, it had been fine—Devon had read a graphic novel, and Rylee had explained in detail how she'd turned her old shorts inside out, cut a straight line up the side seam and then a wedge shape, and first glued, then sewed the piece of lace doily on so it peeked out from the denim.

The next day, Aaliyah had said, "So, Devon seemed kind of . . . not really *into* the whole conversation yesterday?"

Rylee had shrugged. "Shorts aren't her thing."

Aaliyah had made a face. "Oh. Well, she might not want to sit with us today. I brought my sister's *Teen Vogue* for us to look at—just to get some ideas . . ."

"Nice!" Rylee had been thrilled. "She can read a

book—she won't care."

Had Devon cared? Now Rylee wondered, as Mr. Pfister finished his review and started the class on the geometry assignment. She'd never really asked; she'd just told Devon what she and Aaliyah were going to do and apologized that it was going to be boring. It hadn't seemed like Devon had minded. She'd just sat at the end of the table, reading another graphic novel. But as the days had gone on, and Aaliyah always had some other new project—they'd gone from decorating shorts to trying to dye one of Aaliyah's fuzzy fleece slippers when she'd spilled hot sauce on them—Devon had kind of drifted off. One day she'd told Rylee she was going to read in the library, and Rylee had said, "Sure, okay. I'll catch you later!"

And she hadn't, Rylee realized. She and Devon had gone from every-day-plus-weekends friends since fifth grade to wave-in-the-hall sixth-grade acquaintances. Rylee barely remembered seeing Devon at school last year in seventh at all, and now that she was in Rylee's geometry class . . .

Rylee's eyes followed Devon's progress as she returned from Mr. Pfister's desk. Now that Devon was right here, Rylee realized she'd missed her. She'd missed her sincerity, and her funny doodles and notes during class. She'd missed hanging out with someone so easygoing. But having traded Devon's low-key, who-cares-what-you-wear company for Aaliyah's critical fashionista eye, Rylee wondered if Devon would welcome her back.

An old friend who kind of got obsessed with clothes and made new friends is in the class you just transferred to. Is she:

    a. Someone you should confront about being a bad friend

    b. Someone you should expect to apologize to you

    c. Someone you should wave at and act like nothing happened

    d. Someone who is totally dead to you, and you can hate them forever

12

Valued and Respected

"Hey, Devon! Devon, wait up!" Rylee hustled toward her old friend, putting on a friendly smile. "So, hey, I haven't seen you in—"

"Um, hi. My elective's all the way in the library, and I'm going to the bathroom first, so . . ."

"Oh!" Rylee said, quickly falling into step with the other girl. "I just wanted to say hi. I can't believe you're in my geometry section, you math hater!"

Devon shot Rylee an odd look and walked a little faster. "I'm not a math hater. Mrs. Daily just assigned too much homework in sixth, so I didn't feel like taking the test to get out of fundamentals. Last year Mom said I should start practicing putting in more effort since high school grades count toward colleges, so . . ." Devon shrugged.

"Oh. Well, I feel ridiculous," Rylee admitted. She'd been certain Devon had hated math. What else was she misremembering? The bathrooms were just ahead, and Rylee was out of time. "Well, good to see you. . . . Maybe we can talk at lunch?"

"Can't today. I have a club meeting," Devon said, bouncing a little.

"Seriously?" Rylee blurted, surprised again. Devon had never wanted to do things like that in sixth grade. She had been totally antigroup. "Which club? I was thinking—"

"Look, Rylee, I have to *go*," Devon said with heavy emphasis on the last word. "I'll talk to you—"

"Okay, bye," Rylee interrupted brightly, then felt her face heating. *Smooth*.

Devon just gave her another odd look and ducked into the bathroom doorway.

Shoulders hunched in embarrassment, Rylee hurried down the hall in the opposite direction. *Ugh*, that hadn't gone the way she'd wanted it to at all.

Rylee wasn't in any more of a good mood by the time advisory rolled around. That day, Ms. Johnston's room was arranged with the desks in a circle, with the art supplies on the periphery of the room. Rylee mumbled an unenthused "Hey" to Ms. Johnston, then looked at the advisory Question of the Day on the board.

Konnichiwa (Japanese afternoon greeting). Grab a seat and greet the person next to you! In Japan, polite greetings are a big part of the culture and can help people feel acknowledged, valued, and respected. Question of the Day: What is something that makes you feel acknowledged, valued, and respected? Think about it and be ready to share your answer and listen to the answers of your peers before we continue working on our self-portrait projects. Welcome to advisory!

Ugh. Rylee was *not* in the mood for advisory again. She already spent all her free time coiling up strips of paper for her self-portrait project, and now she going to have to try and say "hello" in Japanese? Rylee hesitated before choosing a desk, nearly running into the red-haired boy from the library who was aiming for the same seat. She was surprised when he backed off and sat next to her.

"Guten Tag," he said, and grinned, his braces catching the light.

Rylee blinked. "I *know* that's not how you pronounce the word on the board."

The boy shrugged. "Well, no, but it's basically the same thing, just in German."

Rylee, whose sixth-grade Spanish journey had just barely gotten her past "hola" and, if she thought about it hard, a hesitantly pronounced "¿Dónde está el baño?" just shook her head. "If you say so. Um, hi. Leo," she added, suddenly remembering his name.

"Hey! Konnichiwa, DeNia," the boy said suddenly, leaning forward as DeNia settled on Rylee's other side. "Did you already start on the timeline for Mr. Gil's class?"

"Hey, Leo. Hey, Rylee," DeNia said, digging into her backpack. "And you have to be kidding. We just got that assignment, like, an hour ago."

"I was just checking," Leo teased. "I know how you always want to get a jump on all the homework."

"One time," DeNia said, giving him a mock-fierce look. "I turned in something early one time, and you're going to be on my case about it forever."

Rylee swiveled her gaze between the two. DeNia was . . . different with this Leo guy. They chatted like they'd known each other forever. She hadn't thought DeNia had . . . friends at school, for some reason.

Rylee frowned and found herself just then looking around the circle for Aaliyah, who was sliding into a seat across from them wearing an oversize red, white, and black plaid T-shirt knotted at her waist and black bike shorts. She was talking animatedly to the girl next to her, who was nodding eagerly.

"So, did you get a chance to look at my notes?" DeNia asked, interrupting Rylee's staring.

"Um, yeah, I looked at them." Rylee tried to change the subject. "So, how do you guys know each other? Did you . . . work on a project together or something?" she asked, glancing over at Leo, who had grabbed a rectangle of paper from the stack of multicolored sticky notes Mr. Gil was handing out, and passed the pad to her.

"Yeah, in social studies last year. You recognize Leo, right? From Press Club?"

Rylee hadn't remembered he was also in Press Club, but she nodded anyway. "Right. Um, what do you think we're supposed to do with these?"

DeNia examined the hot-pink rectangle of paper in her hands. "Probably make name tags or something," she said. "So . . . Rylee? What do you think of my plan? If you can make a short questionnaire, we can get it into the first paper, and then the whole school will have a chance to take it. Our junior high is a good sample size for research."

Rylee tucked her foot beneath her and shifted in her seat. "Um, okay, but what if not everybody answers the questionnaire? I still think I should interview some older people, too. Also, I'm glad you want to work on this, DeNia, just, don't get mad if we don't get a perfect grade, okay? I'm not a science genius or anything."

"So? Nobody said I was, either," DeNia said, sounding defensive.

On the other side of her, Leo snort-laughed. "Yeah, right. Has she showed you her science fair stuff? She made this whole spreadsheet on the computer—"

"Did you hear a noise?" DeNia interrupted. "It was really *loud* and *annoying.*"

"Whatever, science genius," Leo said with a little smirk.

"Buenos días, scholars, and welcome to advisory!" Mr. Gil called, and the last stragglers rushed to find seats in the circle. Mr. Gil was squeezing something in his hands that looked like a squishy rubber sea urchin as he smiled. "I'm excited to share two things with you that make me feel valued and respected. One is when someone sees the work that I've done, and acknowledges that I've done a good job, and the other is when someone respects my opinion on a topic and believes I know what I'm talking about. What about you . . . Ms. Johnston?" He gave the ball an underhand toss to the teacher standing next to him.

Ms. Johnston fumbled the ball and laughed a little. "Oh! My turn already! Good afternoon, friends! Two things that make me feel valued and respected are when my family laughs at my jokes, and when people ask me to be a part of a group that's working on an important project. What about you . . . Joya?"

Rylee tried to pay attention, but she was mostly thinking furiously, grateful that she was far on the other side of the circle from where Ms. Johnston had started the ball tossing. She hated questions like this that only *sounded* easy. What did it really mean to be valued—and respected? Was that something you got from your friends? Weren't they just supposed to . . . like you?

Several students said things that were almost word for word what Mr. Gil and Ms. Johnston had said. One boy threw the ball—overhand—to a friend of his across the circle, and Mr. Gil called a time-out and a do-over. The boy had to get up, say what made him feel respected all over again, and pass the ball properly.

Rylee had to fight back giggles when Leo snort-laughed again. Then Rylee tensed as the next student spoke in a confident, friendly voice.

"Hujambo! I'm Aaliyah, and that's how you say 'hi' in Swahili, and two things that make me feel valued and respected are when people respect African American culture, and when people are, like, fair to me."

Rylee's face scrunched like she'd chewed on a mouthful of sand. *She* liked fairness. Too bad Aaliyah didn't always offer that to other people.

And then, Rylee realized that she knew just what she wanted to say when the ball came. It was something she wished she could say to Aaliyah, something that had been boiling inside her ever since Cherise had talked to her in the bathroom at the library. She was on pins and needles as she waited through Leo's slightly sarcastic comments (Leo felt valued and respected when people didn't call him Ginger, Penny, or Red and when people believed him when he said they were smart) and caught the nubbly ball in her outstretched fingers.

"Um, okay. Konnichiwa," Rylee said, pronouncing the word carefully. "I'm Rylee, and two things that make me feel valued and respected are when people want to know something about me, they *ask* instead of making stuff up and talking about me behind my back, which is *rude*." Rylee paused, realizing that her voice had quickly gotten too loud. She cleared her throat, trying to ignore the embarrassed heat making the back of her neck prickle. "Also, I feel valued and respected when people don't laugh at me," she mumbled, and quickly tossed DeNia the ball.

Fortunately, no one had laughed, and while the ball had gone the rest of the way around the circle, Mr. Gil had been writing everyone's "valued and respected" thoughts. Afterward, he read them aloud, then talked about how the goal in advisory was to create a "culture of respect" at school. Knowing the things that made people feel respected and valued—and why—was "of vital importance" to making connections and maintaining friendships.

Rylee selected two new colors of construction paper, pink and magenta, to add to her portrait and wondered if she'd ever even known what made her friends feel respected and valued. She'd never asked—regular friends didn't do that, right? But probably, it would have made Devon feel respected and valued if Rylee had talked to her at lunch and not ignored her. It was okay that she didn't care about fashion, but since Rylee had been her friend, she should have been a better one. It wouldn't have been that hard to bring up things that Devon *did* care about, like art, and movies. Maybe Aaliyah could have found something she liked about those topics if she had tried. Friendship was more than just liking. It was thinking about the friend and *showing* the friend that they were valued.

And Rylee had assumed Aaliyah, at least, had respected her . . . until she didn't.

Turning back to her seat, Rylee almost collided with the subject of her musings.

"Sorry!"

Rylee's apology was automatic, but Aaliyah lurched wildly to the side, avoiding the collision—and Rylee's quiet word. Aaliyah snatched up pink construction paper, jerking a sheet from the stack, then moved on quickly as if choosing the next color was the most important thing in the world—and as if Rylee wasn't even there.

Rylee went back to her seat, frowning a little. Ms. *Be Fair to Me* had been awfully jumpy. She wondered if that was because Aaliyah was remembering how she hadn't been fair to Rylee. That was probably too much to expect, but at least today Rylee had gotten a few things straight in her own head.

For so long, she had been so sad and embarrassed about what had happened at the end-of-year pool party that she'd started acting like *she'd* done something wrong. Rylee had flinched just seeing Aaliyah, and she'd been nervous and intimidated when she'd met Cherise in the bathroom. But *Rylee* wasn't the one who hadn't been fair, who had treated someone as if they didn't have value and didn't deserve respect. All she'd done was go to a party that she had been *invited* to attend. She hadn't done anything wrong.

It was weird how hard that was to remember.

The vacuum cleaner stood stranded in the middle of the front hall, and there was the smell of orange oil and glass cleaner in the air when Rylee opened the front door. Axel, who must have come in just seconds before, was tiptoeing toward the stairs, hoping not to catch Geema's attention. Rylee, who hadn't noticed the smells of housework fast enough, had let the front door close with a thump. She glared silently at Axel who raced away as Geema's voice echoed through the entryway.

"Miss Rylee! That you?"

"Yes, ma'am." Rylee reluctantly followed her Geema's

voice to the front room.

Rylee disliked the front room. It wasn't only the sad fake fireplace (the flames came on when you pushed a button—how was that real?), the dark wood furniture, or the bright aqua-colored rug. She didn't like all the fat blue striped pillows on the couch, or the basket of fancy glass balls on the coffee table, or the blue flowered upholstered chairs that flanked the window, either. Rylee had spent too much time vacuuming and dusting and fluffing that room to like anything about it. It had to be cleaned every single week, even though Geema didn't let anyone play, or eat, or wear shoes, or even sit and read a book in there—unless they were company. Then they could do whatever they wanted, including eat the salted caramels Geema kept in a tightly lidded glass dish that Rylee wasn't even allowed to open.

Geema, wearing a cotton scarf tied over her rollers and an old T-shirt of Daddy Warren's, looked up from where she was buffing a shine onto the coffee table.

"There you are. Do you have homework?"

"Yes, ma'am," Rylee said hopefully. She'd *so* much rather do geometry than dust.

"Finish it up as fast as you can," Geema said, "then come on down to the kitchen. Folks will be here for coffee around six, and you can put out some cake plates and napkins for me."

"What folks?" Rylee asked, peeling out of her sweatshirt. She'd gotten a tiny spot of ink on her white dress and had decided to cover it up. It hadn't been as cute, but at least she hadn't looked sloppy.

"The folks answering your questions. For your little newspaper," Geema clarified when Rylee still looked confused. "You asked me this morning to ask Ms. Grace . . . ?"

"Oh! *Oh!*" Rylee gasped, eyes widening. "Wait, Geema, they're coming *here*!? They're coming to our house? *Tonight!?* But—!"

"But what?" Geema asked, frowning. "Didn't you want to ask your questions?"

"I did! I do! But I thought . . . maybe I could do it on the phone, or something," Rylee said awkwardly. "I . . . they're all coming *here*. Tonight. Okay." Rylee chewed on her bottom lip as her heart raced. "Great," she managed, her voice strangled.

Geema gave the table one last swipe and straightened with a satisfied nod. "They'll be here before you know it, so get a move on, girl. Time's a-wastin'."

"I'm going, I'm going," Rylee said, running for the stairs.

In her room, Rylee gasped for breath as a wave of panic crashed down over her head. "It's all taken care of," Geema had said that morning, but Rylee just hadn't realized how seriously Geema had meant it. The guests were taken care of, but Rylee hadn't picked which questions to ask. She hadn't decided if she wanted to ask young people the same questions as the old people. She and DeNia had just figured out how to work together, and what if DeNia had wanted to help with this part? Was she going to be mad? Rylee didn't know what she was even *doing*.

Ugh! Journalism was just supposed to be something she did so she wouldn't have to see Nevaeh and Aaliyah! And now everything was so stressful! This whole project thing was a *disaster*.

13

Old School, New Rules

Fact: nobody had ever died just from walking into a room full of old people.

Evidence: Rylee had met almost all of Geema's friends before, and she was still standing.

Reasoning: despite the fact that Geema had set this up for that night, and even though Ms. Grace had just swept in from the front porch with her husband, Mr. Shabazz, and two *more* older ladies that Rylee had never even seen, this wasn't going to be a total disaster.

Maybe.

Ms. Margery ("just call me Grandma Marge, honey") was a round, smiling lady with bright red hair that was white at the roots, long red nails, and hardly any wrinkles on her light, freckled skin. Mrs. Paulson, who reminded Rylee she had skipped prayer meeting to come and answer her questions, wore a blue cardigan and matching filmy scarf wrapped around her iron-gray waves, and had skin like a softly wrinkled brown paper bag.

When Daddy Warren's friend Mr. Winslow showed up in a sweater-vest and bow tie, his bald head shining, Rylee texted DeNia in a panic.

Rylee: Halp! Geema invited the WORLD to do friendship interviews.

DeNia's response came quickly.

DeNia: Really? Cool! Are these your old ppl? How many? How old?

Rylee: IDK, six or eight, might be more. And I'm not asking age!!!

DeNia: DOOO IT!!! Get all the deets for a good article!! ASK!!!! It's for SCIENCE!!

Rylee winced, imagining how that would go. Geema was seventy-something, Rylee knew, but Geema also said she was twenty-nine every single year on her birthday.

Rylee: Ugh, fine, I'll ask. TTYL.

DeNia: Good luck!!!! Oh—snap some pics for the article, kthx.

Rylee stood uncertainly in the entrance of the front room, looking at the expectant faces smiling her way. Daddy Warren had dragged in extra chairs, and everyone was waiting for Rylee to tell them why they were there. Ms. Essie from next door had ducked in at the last minute, and Rylee couldn't help but smile at the woman's encouraging thumbs-up.

"Um, thank you, everyone, for being willing to help me with my journalism project," she began.

"Speak up, darlin'," Daddy Warren boomed from the back of the room.

Rylee felt her heat creeping up her neck. She cleared her throat and started again. "Thank you for coming. For journalism class, I'm researching friendship and writing a science article about it. I'll be interviewing people of all ages about the friends they had growing up, and what's different about having friends now, and . . . stuff. There aren't any right answers, so just . . . answer what you think."

Rylee took a step back. Then, remembering something one of her teachers might have said, she added, "Please take a pad of paper and a pen from the table and write your name and, um, age. There are ten questions, and your answers are mostly going to be either *A*, *B*, *C*, or *D*. Just write a letter next to the number, or write 'Yes' or 'No.'"

"Ooh, this is just like school," Ms. Grace said happily. "I was *good* at school."

"This isn't like school," Geema said, rolling her eyes. "There isn't a right answer."

"There is always a right answer," Mrs. Paulson interjected.

Grandma Marge chuckled. "Is that so?"

"Also, I'm recording this," Rylee said, raising her voice a little, "so I can write exactly what you say for the article if you give me any quotes. And before everyone goes home, I need a picture of our group, if that's okay."

"And when is this article coming out?" Mr. Winslow asked, looking at Rylee over his reading glasses. "Where do we get copies of the newspaper?"

"Oh, I'll stop by the school and get a stack," Ms. Grace assured him. "My son-in-law is on the school board."

Aaliyah's dad was on the school board? Rylee felt her stomach clench. Between Ms. Grace and *Aaliyah's* father, there was a 0 percent chance Aaliyah wasn't going to hear about this survey. *Ugh*, and she would probably think it was the most cringey project ever, and then pretend to be nice and ask Rylee questions about it.

She did *not* want to deal with this.

"Well, somebody give me a pen," Daddy Warren said loudly, reaching for one of the spiral notebooks on the table. "Let's get started so we can get to the coffee and cake."

Since Geema had surprised her with interviewees, Rylee was using some of her old questions. She hadn't wanted to ask the older people exactly the same questions she'd asked Mom—especially not the question inspired by Geema and Ms. Grace—but she'd realized the questions mattered less than getting the old people talking about the past, and hopefully from their comments she'd be able to tell if *most* of their friendships had lasted through junior high into high school, or if just some of them had, and if it was about the same between younger people and older people. For the first time since the project had officially started, Rylee was feeling excited.

"All right, this one is 'Yes' or 'No,'" she said, clearing her throat. "Are you still friends with your first friend?"

But as the questions went on, Rylee quickly realized that it was a good thing she'd turned on the voice recorder on her phone. It seemed like every question required ten minutes of discussion by the entire group.

"Wait, what do you mean, do I *believe* in best friends? Regina, what does she mean?"

"Warren, let the child *tell* you," Geema said, sounding exasperated. "Rylee, honey, what do you mean by that?"

Rylee blinked. "Is that one confusing? I just mean, do you believe people have or should have best friends, that's all."

"Well, the Lord is *my* best friend," Mrs. Paulson announced.

"Lizbeth, we are talking about human beings," Mr. Winslow objected. "And I know you and Sister Dials have been thick as thieves ever since she asked you to make your twice-baked potato casserole for the Memorial Day brunch."

"That casserole is something else," Grandma Marge agreed. "I might be best friends with you if you made some for my brunch."

"Does she share recipes?" Ms. Essie was asking Geema in a low voice. "You know Lane loves a good casserole."

"If we say we're her friends, do we still get this casserole? That's what I'm trying to find out," Daddy Warren said, and Mr. Winslow slapped his knee, cackling.

"Oh, you all stop it," Mrs. Paulson said, looking pleased.

"Ahem," Rylee said. "Number Five: What ended your last friendship? What did you learn from it?"

Geema smirked. "Ooh, Gracie, remember Vanessa Moore from senior year?"

Ms. Grace gave Geema a dirty look and sucked her teeth, her expression so much like Aaliyah's when she was mad that Rylee found herself leaning back.

Geema only snickered.

"Humph," Ms. Grace said.

"Say, Roland? Who's Vanessa?" Daddy Warren asked Mr. Shabazz in a loud whisper.

"Just write the answer to the question, Warren Swanson. We can't keep this child up past her bedtime on a school night," Ms. Grace said in a tone of voice meant to shut everyone up.

It mostly worked, except for Geema, whose suppressed laughter came out as a strangled snort. Daddy Warren turned a guffaw into a cough, and Mr. Shabazz elbowed him, chortling.

Rylee looked from one face to another, slightly disbelieving. Rylee knew Geema was silly a lot, and liked to have a good time, but it was so *weird* seeing Ms. Grace, who was always dressed up and did serious things like run a women's club at her church and go to symphony fundraisers, getting teased. Geema didn't treat Ms. Grace like she was a serious person at all. Rylee wondered if she and her friends would still be clowning each other about school when they were in their seventies. Was that what happened when you kept your friends for years? How did people do that?

Though it took an hour and a half to get through only ten questions and take a couple of pictures, in the end, Rylee decided it had been worth it. While she collected the survey responses, Geema brought out an icing-drizzled pound cake and coffee, which Mom and Axel somehow sensed from all the way upstairs and arrived to investigate. After that, the noise level rose, with everyone talking and laughing at once.

Ms. Essie pulled Rylee aside for a brief hug, then stepped back, beaming. "Those were such smart questions, Rylee!"

"Thank you," Rylee said, pleased and embarrassed all at once. She'd been so afraid everyone would know how unprepared she was.

"I got to answer a few of them," Mom was saying, giving Rylee a proud look. "She asked some that really challenged me."

Rylee wandered around the room, smiling in a daze of relief that it was *over*. She found her grandfather pouring himself a cup of coffee, guarding the remains of the cake.

"Daddy Warren? Was the question about best friends too confusing? Should I change it?"

Her grandfather was shaking his head before she finished the sentence. "Naw, don't worry about it," he said. "I understood, when I thought about it a second." He regarded Rylee thoughtfully. "You know your grandma, she could talk a split log into a fence post, but I have just about two or three folks I can spend the time of day with. I don't believe it'd be fair to call any one of them the 'best,' not when all of them are the type of folks who are good to have around whether you need an extra pair of hands or you just want to shoot the breeze for a while. So, that's what I put down on that paper," Daddy Warren said with a decisive nod. "I don't believe in this 'best' business."

"Now, wait just a minute, there. Best friends are *magical*," Ms. Grace interrupted, prodding Daddy Warren with a finger. "You men might not talk about things like we women do, but I'm sure I wouldn't know what to do if I didn't have my nearest and dearest to hold my secrets. You just don't understand best friendship, Warren Swanson; that's what's wrong with you."

Daddy Warren grinned and said something teasing right back to Ms. Grace like he always did, while Rylee backed away from the conversation, her stomach souring. Even though Ms. Grace was only joking, Rylee had a sinking suspicion that *she* was the one who didn't actually understand. Even when she had spent all her time with Devon, Rylee hadn't felt anything *magical*. Maybe she was just doing friendship wrong.

Rylee was almost on the edge of the room when Mrs. Paulson intercepted her.

"Don't let them fill your head with this 'magical' nonsense," the older lady said sternly. "Friendship is nothing but hard work, and don't you forget it."

"Yes, ma'am. Work," repeated Rylee uncertainly, shooting a quick glance around the room. Mrs. Paulson was as starchy and unsmiling as she had been when she'd come into the house, and Rylee didn't want to talk to her. Where was Geema to save her?

"It is work," Mrs. Paulson repeated. "There's nothing magical about it. Why, it's work to be worth trusting. It's work to treat others as you'd like them to treat you. It's work to see other people as they really are, and it's work sometimes to let folks see the real you."

Surprised, Rylee turned more fully to face the woman, wishing that she hadn't switched off the recorder when she'd finished asking the survey questions. "I . . . wow. Yeah, that's really true. I like that."

Rylee couldn't get over it. Instead of giving terrible, sour advice like someone who'd never had a friend, Mrs. Paulson sounded . . . wise. Rylee realized she'd assumed Mrs. Paulson's unsmiling face went with an unfriendly heart.

"It's also work to hear what your friends need to say to you, and work to be brave enough to speak your piece when you need to," Ms. Essie said, moving to join their conversation from where she'd been sitting on one of the flowered armchairs. "Mrs. Paulson is so right, Rylee. It's work to listen and be accepting, if your friends make choices you wouldn't." She glanced at Mrs. Paulson. "Especially when they might have beliefs that you don't share, or like things you don't like. It takes a lot of working on *you*—to be your best self. But you know, the payoff is worth it. People are friends because having someone who gets you is worth everything."

Mrs. Paulson's smile was small but visible. She patted Rylee's arm and stepped back. "Yes, indeed," she said. "I look forward to reading your journalism, young lady. Thank you for inviting me to take part in this evening."

"Oh, no, thank you for coming, Mrs. Paulson," Rylee said, truly meaning it this time. She couldn't believe how she hadn't even wanted to *do* this interview thing. What if she hadn't asked Geema to help her? She would have missed so much. Rylee almost wished she could rewind the whole evening and start over without being nervous or too freaked out to enjoy the history and the stories sitting in the front room with her.

"We haven't been introduced, but I'm Essie Rockwell; I live next door," Ms. Essie was saying as Rylee turned to go. "My partner, Lane, is an amateur foodie, and I love to bring recipes home for them to try out. Are you willing to share your twice-baked potato casserole recipe with me in return for my spinach-artichoke-lasagna recipe? I promise you it's excellent, and even my carnivore friends enjoy it."

"Elizabeth Paulson; how nice to meet you, Ms. Rockwell. I am happy to swap recipes, but I admit, I'm mostly curious. Whatever started you putting artichokes in a lasagna?"

"Oh, please call me Essie . . ."

Rylee glanced back and smiled. In her black boots

and jeans, Ms. Essie was tall, broad-shouldered, and striking, with choppy, short, dyed burgundy hair, a full-sleeve tattoo of a mermaid on her right arm, and tons of smile lines. Mrs. Paulson was short and bony, and her cardigan was draped around her narrow shoulders even though the evening was warm. The two ladies couldn't be more different.

But maybe that didn't matter.

Two ladies who are different ages and different races meet at a neighbor's house for coffee. Are they:

    a. Only talking to each other to be polite

    b. Bonding over a love of cooking

    c. Wondering about what makes the other person who they are

    d. Going to take a chance on finding out what they have in common

The *Segrest Sentinel* Reports

FRIENDSHIP: Old-School-Style

by Rylee Swanson

***

As part of the activities of Press Club, this year eighth graders DeNia Alonso and Rylee Swanson are conducting a scientific journalism project about friendship. Throughout the semester, they will be reporting on different aspects of friendship and how it affects those of us in junior high.

***

In 2015, scientists, including Dr. Amy C. Hartl of Florida Atlantic University, gave surveys to 410 seventh graders and asked them the same questions once every year until they were high school seniors. Dr. Hartl learned that about half the friendships of those middle school students didn't last through even one school year (1306–7). To see if the results of a study like this might have been different back in the day, Rylee Swanson conducted an informal survey

176

of her grandparents and their friends.

We can't find out the same information from talking to only a few older people, but of the nine adults between the ages of 35 and 74 interviewed, two of them were still friends with people they met in seventh grade, three of them hadn't seen them in years but still sent holiday cards, and two of them said they definitely did not have friends from seventh grade. The other respondents said they couldn't remember what happened in seventh grade because it was "a long time ago."

The older people interviewed did not think it was unusual for people to still be friends with people they had met in seventh grade. The two respondents who were definitely still friends with their seventh-grade friends also said that they were "best" friends with people they had known since elementary school. This turned the discussion to best friends. Some seemed to believe that best friends aren't a big deal, or that having a few good friends is ideal. Advice about friendship was offered by Elizabeth Paulson, who claimed that all friendship is hard work.

"It is work to be worth trusting, and to trust people. Sometimes the hardest work is letting people see who you really are," Paulson commented. The hard work of friendship might be one of the reasons that junior high friendships don't last forever, especially when sometimes it is hard to be who we are, or to let others know the real person inside us.

Segrest School: What do *you* think?

Students, faculty, and staff are invited to visit the *Segrest Sentinel* online and click on the survey link. The ten-question Friendship Survey is there. It will take you only about two minutes to fill it out, and then we'll add your answers to the answers of everyone in the school who takes it. You have until October 3 to take part in the survey. We hope that this survey will help us ask ourselves better questions about how friendships work and how we can be and make better friends this year.

The *Segrest Sentinel* staff offers special

thanks to Warren and Regina Swanson, Ms. Jayna Swanson, Ms. Essie Rockwell, Roland and Grace Shabazz, Dr. Margery Cope, Mrs. Elizabeth Paulson, and Mr. Robert Winslow for their help in taking our friendship survey.

Works Cited

Hartl, Amy C., et al. "A Survival Analysis of Adolescent Friendships: The Downside of Dissimilarity." *Psychological Science*, vol. 26, no. 8, 2015, pp. 1304-15.

14

Refriending

DeNia was gushing the next morning as she looked at the pictures on Rylee's phone.

"You got such good data," DeNia said, doing a happy dance in her seat. "This is going to be amazing! I wish we could get some of my dad's friends together to do this. I bet some of their answers would be really, really different than my mom's friends," DeNia added, forehead wrinkling in thought. "You know, if we planned it right, we could—"

"We can't," Rylee blurted, feeling a little panicky at the idea of doing an evening of surveys with DeNia's parents. "I mean," she explained, when DeNia gave her a startled look, "we have to concentrate on the students at Segrest, right? If we keep adding people, we're never going to finish, and remember, we're on a deadline . . . ?"

"Right, right," DeNia said, and sighed. "I was just wishing out loud, that's all. I can't wait to get to high school where I can do more stuff like this."

I can, Rylee thought to herself. Just thinking about high school made Rylee tired. With all the friend troubles she'd had this year, imagining having to do it all again was just too much to contemplate.

As she entered Mr. Pfister's class later that morning, Rylee set her ukulele case and backpack next to her usual spot and dropped her homework in Mr. Pfister's box as other students streamed around her noisily, talking—or frantically trying to finish the geometry assignment. Last week, Mr. Blaine had been proctoring some kind of test, so the library had been closed during lunch. Press Club and everyone else had been forced into the bright, noisy, social space of the cafeteria. Rylee had been deeply grateful for the other library lunchers filling the empty tables near the exit. Even though the Spite Sisters hadn't even noticed she was there—probably—Rylee had been extremely uncomfortable to be back where her friendship with them had begun. She wondered, not for the first time, what she would have done this year without pushy, friendly, frustrating, stubborn DeNia. Rylee smiled to herself, picturing DeNia's excitement over their latest article. When she didn't feel like she was being dragged behind a bullet train, working with DeNia was really cool. No one else—

"So, hey," Devon said, plopping down in the desk across the aisle from her.

"Oh. Hey! Hi!" Rylee had never been so glad Mr. Pfister didn't like seating charts. She curled her toes in her shoes to stop herself from leaping up from her seat, grabbing Devon by the collar, and screaming, *Don't move! You have to let me fix our friendship!* She had to act normally, or at least try, so she wouldn't freak Devon out completely.

"How are you?" Rylee's voice cracked.

Devon was twisting the hem of her T-shirt between her fingers. "I'm good. So, we kind of got interrupted yesterday?" Her voice went up in a hesitant question.

"Um . . . yeah." Rylee couldn't even remember what she'd wanted to ask. "I'm *so* glad you're talking to me," she blurted, then winced at Devon's immediately unhappy expression. "Sorry," she muttered, reminding herself not to be weird.

A boy landed in the seat in front of Devon with a

clatter of books. He gave Rylee a disinterested glance and surreptitiously pulled out his phone.

"No, Rylee, *I'm* sorry." Devon leaned closer and dropped her voice. "It was really cruddy of me to be jealous that you had other friends, and then I stopped talking to you. I was so mad, and then . . . you were still nice, but I started hanging around in the tutoring room after school, so we didn't walk home at the same time, and then you weren't around at all anymore, and then the school year was over, and I felt really, really stupid."

Rylee stared, shocked, as Devon gulped and twisted her shirt harder. Devon had vanished on *purpose*!? Rylee felt a little embarrassed that she hadn't even considered that.

"I'm so sorry you felt that way," Rylee said, then glared across the aisle at the boy who had put his phone away and who was now clearly eavesdropping. She got up from her seat and knelt in front of Devon's desk, lowering her voice. "I wish so much I had made different choices. I shouldn't have gotten so into Aaliyah that I didn't leave time for you. I want to—"

"Good *morning*!" Mr. Pfister's voice boomed cheerfully, and both Rylee and Devon jumped. "I sure hope I have yesterday's assignment from everyone in the

183

basket already, because anything turned in thirty seconds from now is *late* and worth half the points. Ooh, we've got a few runners today. In honor of those who just finished their assignment, why don't we start with a little five-question quiz? Take out a sheet of paper, folks." Mr. Pfister raised his voice over the groans. "Oh, come on! You did the homework—you've got this!"

Rylee and Devon exchanged exasperated looks. Teachers! Why were they always so loud and in the way when important conversations were going on? Grumping to herself, Rylee slumped back in her seat and prepared her brain for lines and angles.

Rylee was scribbling the last equation on her notes when Mr. Pfister finally dismissed the class. This time Devon waited while Rylee grabbed her things.

"Is that a violin?" Devon asked, eyeing the case Rylee hitched across her shoulder.

"Nope, a ukulele. One of my electives is chorus— but it's a ukulele chorus this quarter."

"That is so cool!" Devon exclaimed. "I wish I'd known it wasn't going to be singing the whole time. I wouldn't have signed up for yearbook."

"Why not, though? You used to like to take pictures, right?" Rylee hitched her bag onto her shoulder.

Though Rylee was certain Devon loved taking pictures, she'd been wrong about the Devon of her memories before, so she made the words a question.

"The taking pictures part is fine," Devon said, falling into step with Rylee as they walked down the hall. "I actually like yearbook okay. But we're learning this layout program, and it's really fiddly. Maddalena and Fallon are the only ones who know what they're doing, so they end up helping everyone. We have to write words to go with the pictures, and everything I write sounds totally cheesy. And you know how Mrs. Goins makes you rewrite everything all the time."

Rylee grimaced, remembering their sixth-grade English language arts teacher. "Yeah, she is kind of picky. Well, at least you get to take pictures?"

Devon grinned. "Yep. And some of them are going to be on-screen for Wednesday Forum. So, that's cool."

"That is really cool," Rylee agreed, impressed. "You'll have to show me which pics are yours."

"You'll have to show me how to play ukulele someday," Devon replied.

"Deal."

As they came to the corner of the hall where Rylee needed to turn toward the arts building, she hesitated. This had been so easy. She and Devon had picked up chatting like they hadn't ever taken a break, but . . .

"Um . . . so, Devon, did you want to, um, meet me by the bike rack after school?"

"I want to, yeah, but I have, uh, something going on before I go home." Devon shifted, rubbing the back of her neck awkwardly. "Can I text you later?"

"Oh, sure, no problem," Rylee said, backpedaling. Obviously, Devon had other friends. It wasn't like Rylee had expected them to wait for each other or trade off having snacks and doing homework at each other's houses like they had in sixth grade. "We don't have to get together at all. I just thought, you know, if you, um, weren't doing anything—"

"I have Mouse Guard," Devon blurted, and almost glared at Rylee, her expression fierce.

"You have . . . what now?" Rylee asked. "Mouse . . . ?"

"Mouse Guard. It's a game," Devon explained, the skin on her neck going blotchy. "I'm game master, and everybody is in the guard and we have to do stuff to protect this village"— Devon's voice was picking up speed—"but we only have two hours to play and Tuesdays are the only day everyone can come in person because Cameron has to watch their cousins after school, and Maddalena has chorus on Thursdays, and Danya has synagogue on Saturdays, and Hebrew school on Sundays, so Mom said we could play during the week, but if I wanted to have friends over after school I had to work harder so I didn't fall behind, so now I have tutoring on Mondays so I can be in geometry."

Rylee replayed the last few pieces of Devon's massive run-on sentence until she understood it.

"Oh. Oh! Okay. Well, text me after the game." Rylee walked backward a few feet toward the arts building. "Mouse Guard, huh? That sounds cool. Is it a graphic novel, or did you make it up? Is that what a game master does? Is it one of those games with, like, ten million weird dice? Oh! I think Cameron sits next to me at Wednesday Forum—always in a sweatshirt, right? And was Maddalena the tall girl with the long braids and glasses that sat next to the aquarium in sixth grade?"

Devon opened her mouth to answer when Mr. Blaine turned the corner and nearly mowed her down. "Excuse me! Sorry about that."

Devon staggered, then straightened. "I'm okay, Mr. Blaine."

"Get to class, girls; passing period is almost over, and you don't want to be late."

"Why isn't there ever any time to talk?" Devon

complained as Mr. Blaine hurried off toward the library.

Rylee just . . . smiled. That was exactly what she'd been thinking. "Have fun at yearbook. Text me."

"I will," Devon said, digging in her backpack.

Rylee turned away and jogged up the hallway a few feet before she heard Devon yell, *"Byeeeeee!"*

Laughing, Rylee swiveled back to see Devon's camera raised. She grinned and waved. Something warm unraveled inside her chest, like a sunflower had opened and spread its petals to bask in golden light.

"I agree with DeNia this time," Ms. Johnston said the next afternoon, tilting her head as she read through the full list of Rylee's haphazard list of questions. "I like the list you used for the elders in your community, and I think these types of questions will pull some really good responses from every single one of the students and staff at our school. You are inviting teachers and staff members to take part as well, aren't you?"

Rylee shot a quick glance at DeNia, whose face lit up. "Well . . . you don't think it will be too many people?"

"No, I told you," DeNia burst out. "You can never

get too much data. If you're a good writer, I bet you could get all three of your articles out of this," she continued, turning to face Ms. Johnston. "A feature about interviewing the oldies"—at Ms. Johnston's arched brow, DeNia corrected herself—"I mean, elders. And then, a science article about their surveys, and how you can't generalize from that small of a sample size, but what questions you'd look for if you had more older people to talk to or something.

"The last one could be the one Ms. Johnston assigned us," DeNia continued, looking at Rylee again. "That's the one where we talk about the answers we got, and how we chose the questions, and what we hope people will learn from our research."

"I think you can get one more article out of this," Ms. Johnston interjected. "What if you interviewed each other? Since this is the first time the two of you have collaborated on an article, how did that work? Did it bring you closer to work on a project together, or was it hard on your friendship? How did your own friendship get started? That sounds like a human-interest article, doesn't it? Is it hard working with a friend?"

"Well—" DeNia began.

"Except, we're not really friends, though," Rylee

cut in. She turned to DeNia, expecting her to agree, then flinched at DeNia's stricken expression. DeNia wiped the hurt from her face so quickly that Rylee almost didn't believe she'd seen it, but of course she had. Even though DeNia was only someone she talked about work with, *Rylee* would feel the same sting if DeNia basically blurted out that she didn't really like her.

"Sorry, I mean, we're not *not* friends," Rylee said quickly, hoping her bright smile would help delete her thoughtless words. "DeNia is super nice, and very, *very* smart, but we don't, really, like, know-*know* each other? We just kind of . . . met, since we sat next to each other in homeroom this semester, and then she made me join Press Club, so we're, um, just, like, seat-friends? And we're working together, so that's making us project-friends. And—"

"That's perfect," Ms. Johnston said generously, giving both girls a smile. "You definitely have something to write about—including a definition of friendship from each of you. People really use the word 'friend' in a lot of different ways, don't they? We know how 'friend' is used on social media platforms. But, are those our real friends? Do they really 'like' us when they 'like' our posts? Are there rules for how long you have to hang out with someone before they're a real friend? Those are the kinds of questions I thought about when I was growing up."

"Right," Rylee said, feeling sweat prickling in her armpits. She flicked a glance over at DeNia, who was sitting with her arms crossed and her face blank. "Exactly."

"Why don't the two of you work on interview questions for each other right now?" Ms. Johnston encouraged. "That's a quick space-filler for the sidebar that we'll count as one of your three articles this issue. We'll use it to introduce you as the creators of this science journalism project, and then people can follow your bylines. Sound good?"

Both Rylee and DeNia nodded.

When Ms. Johnston walked away, Rylee cleared her throat and gathered her courage to apologize. "Hey, I—"

"Right, so we can start with five interview questions," DeNia interrupted, taking out her laptop. She woke up the screen and swiped and tapped until she opened a document. "Let's just write them, then we can swap computers and answer them, and boom, done. We'll turn in our first articles today. Okay?"

"DeNia—" Rylee began again.

"Great." DeNia bent over her keyboard and started to work.

Perfect. Rylee squeezed her eyes closed, wishing she could fall into a hole. She really hadn't meant to hurt DeNia's feelings. Could she never stop messing up this friend thing?

15

Unacceptable Option

Rylee watched the leaves swirling across the road in the wake of a passing car and rubbed her arms. It was unexpectedly chilly this morning, and across the sky, high white clouds feathered in wispy lines. She was wearing a thick red pullover, denim cutoffs, black-and-gray striped tights, and her favorite stompy black boots, having only half listened to Daddy Warren the night before, saying something about a storm coming in by the weekend. It had been sunny, then cloudy, and then sunny again so far, and she'd only been walking for ten minutes. Rylee really hoped it wouldn't rain while she was walking to school.

Despite writing out questions for their friendship

survey, seeing DeNia every morning in homeroom and most lunch periods at Press Club, the two of them hadn't really gotten a chance to talk much. The first edition of the *Segrest Sentinel* was almost ready to be "put to bed," as Ms. Johnston called it, so everyone was running around, panicking to get their three articles, quizzes, or interviews as polished as possible before the deadline. The editor, a tall, big eighth grader named Nate, wore black-rimmed glasses, had bushy, intimidating eyebrows, and was a lot stricter than Rylee had expected. He'd given her back the article she'd written about Geema's friends and told her she needed to "make it tighter." And then he smiled. With teeth.

When Rylee had gone to Ms. Johnston for help, the teacher had suggested she cut the number of words that ended in *y*, like "very" or "really" or "actually." Rylee was surprised the sentences still made sense after she'd deleted almost all the adverbs, but at least when she'd returned it, Nate hadn't given her that scary smile again.

With the wind pushing her, Rylee joined the crowd of elementary students at the crosswalk, waiting for the crossing guard to hold up her sign and lead them across the two-lane road to the elementary school to the right, and Segrest, which was down the block to the left. No longer the tallest in a sea of elementary students, Rylee was happy to see a group of taller students ahead, and to recognize Devon's camouflage jacket and chaotic curls.

Rylee called to her. "Hey! Dev!"

Devon turned and waved just as the crowd began to move. She slowed so Rylee could reach her, calling, "Are you early, or am I late?" as she walked backward a few steps to hear Rylee's reply.

"You're not supposed to walk like that," one of the elementary girls announced loudly. "You're not being safe."

Devon rolled her eyes and turned around.

"I'm early," Rylee said, stepping around the younger girl and falling into step beside her friend as they crossed the zebra stripe on the road. "It's so cold I practically ran."

Devon laughed. "Those are cute tights, but yeah, I definitely wouldn't have worn shorts today. It's supposed to freeze tonight."

"Oh, well," Rylee sighed, tucking her hands into her armpits. "If it gets really bad, I can always put on my gym T-shirt under my sweater, I guess."

"I might have a vest or something in my PE locker,"

Devon offered. Before Rylee could take her up on that—or figure out a way to ask politely if it was camouflage—someone shouted behind them.

"Hey, friends!"

A girl with shaggy, chin-length hair waved at them from the fence at the corner of the school lot. Devon sped up and pulled Rylee forward as the girl's long-legged stride shortened the distance between them.

"You remember Madd," Devon said by way of introduction, and Rylee smiled, remembering the serious-faced girl in sixth grade with the waist-length braids.

"Hey, Maddalena," she said. So, this was one of Devon's mouse game players. Aaliyah had once said that Maddy looked like an escapee from *Prairie Lotus*, a book they'd read for a social studies project, and with her long, straight, black hair, Maddalena *had* looked a little like she could be Hanna, the Chinese American girl who had emigrated to the prairie in the 1880s. Rylee scrutinized Maddalena's dark jeans, chunky-soled leather loafers, and cute backpack purse. Eighth-grade Maddalena was definitely not channeling the Hanna-on-the-prairie look anymore.

"Hey, Rylee." Maddalena flashed her a quick smile and turned back to Devon, pulling a rolled-up piece of paper from her pack. "Okay, so I drew another picture of the map that shows where the merchant train was going," she said. "I think it's better than my last one, because it shows more of the terrain. We can just tape it down—"

Rylee listened, bemused, as the two girls began discussing bits of their game. Devon stopped once, apologetically, but Rylee interrupted her explanation. "No, it's not boring. It sounds really detailed, like a movie."

"There *is* a movie, and comic books," Maddalena said approvingly, and the girls went back to their discussion.

Rylee would have gone on listening to them as they walked up to the main entrance of Segrest, except she saw something that made her insides freeze. Standing in the front hall beside the founder's photograph (Dr. Maria Segrest, 1979) was Aaliyah—and DeNia! As Rylee watched, DeNia smiled up at Aaliyah like she was a friend, not someone who hid in closets and *laughed* at people.

Rylee's mouth dropped open in horror as Aaliyah dug into her backpack and handed DeNia a gift bag, sweeping back her long braids and looking pleased with herself as DeNia glanced up at her. As Aaliyah gestured, DeNia looked inside the bag, and then laughed.

Rylee's stomach was as heavy as if she'd swallowed Daddy Warren's barbells.

Why was Aaliyah Green talking to DeNia? What did she want? Wasn't DeNia the kind of girl Aaliyah normally would have said was "a little *much*"? Aaliyah wouldn't talk to DeNia without a reason—a really nasty, really mean, really Spite Sisters kind of reason. What was she planning to do once DeNia thought she liked her? Would she invite her to a party and humiliate her, too?

"Ry? Rylee?" Rylee hadn't realized she had stopped walking until Devon said her name. She was a few steps ahead, looking back with a frown. "Aren't you coming?"

"Um, yeah. I'm coming," Rylee said, trying to smile.

When she looked back up, DeNia and Aaliyah were moving down the hallway, joining the mass of students pouring through the corridor. Rylee said a quick good-bye to Devon, mumbling something about geometry, and hurried to homeroom with a sense of foreboding. Up ahead, she could still see DeNia and Aaliyah walking, side by side, toward Ms. Johnston's room. Rylee imagined the question on her survey:

One of the Spite Sisters is giving presents to a girl you're doing a journalism project with, but who you said wasn't really your friend. Do you:

   a. Accept that bad things happen, and
      pretend you didn't see anything

   b. Tell the Spite Sister to step off because
      she's messing with your (kind of) friend

   c. Ask your other friend what's going on, and
      if she knows how awful the Spite Sister is

   d. Have no right to ask anyone anything,
      since neither of them are really your
      friends

Rylee was relieved to see DeNia at her desk as usual in homeroom, pulling out her science textbook and a piece of paper. Rylee hurried forward, then hovered awkwardly. She didn't know what to say.

"Good morning, Rylee! What a cozy-looking sweater," Ms. Johnston said, coming up the aisle behind her. She smiled in thanks as DeNia glanced up at Rylee's outfit.

"Hey," DeNia said vaguely.

"Hi, DeNia." Rylee sat, grateful Ms. Johnston had kind of broken the ice, so DeNia had said something. Rylee rubbed her still-cold hands and fiddled with her backpack. She didn't know any other way to start but to just . . . start. She shot a quick glance behind her.

No one was listening, but she still dropped her voice.

"Um . . . so you're friends with Aaliyah Washington?"

DeNia kept copying whatever out of her science book. "No."

That was . . . unexpected. Rylee rolled the edge of her cardigan between her fingers. "Okay," she said, smoothing the knitted fringe. "I, um, I saw she gave you a present this morning?"

DeNia looked up, her expression blank. "So?"

Obviously, this wasn't going to work. DeNia didn't owe her details, especially after Rylee's "we're not friends" comment the other day, which obviously still had DeNia feeling some kind of way. But Rylee couldn't just drop it, not if she cared even a little bit about DeNia. Aaliyah wasn't how she seemed to be, and people needed to know.

Rylee rubbed her forehead, and mumbled quickly, *"Sheusedtobemyfriend."*

DeNia kept writing. *"Duh.* You ate lunch with her all the time last year."

Rylee kept her eyes on the desktop and repeated herself slowly. "She used to be my friend . . . but then she and some other people pranked me." She looked up at DeNia, then looked away again, trying to carefully choose her words. "I . . . I didn't expect . . . just . . . DeNia, if you hang out with her, she isn't . . . um. Sometimes it's hard. To hang out with her. That's all."

Finally dropping her pen, DeNia opened her mouth, closed it, and studied Rylee in silence for a moment. "Huh," she said finally, and went back to her science book.

While she sat there wondering what to say next, Ms. Johnston aimed her remote at the flat screen on the wall and started the Segrest School Morning Show.

Rylee crossed her arms over her churning middle, feeling like there had been an earthquake and she had been knocked off her foundation. DeNia hadn't even *said* anything except *huh*. Didn't she care?

If someone had tried to warn Rylee about Aaliyah, would she have listened?

Across the aisle, DeNia dropped her pencil. Rylee startled when she saw a square of paper being kicked into the aisle near her foot. Rylee placed her foot on the paper and waited until Ms. Johnston picked up a stack of papers on the corner of her desk.

Not that it's your business, but:
  1. The Washingtons live across the street from us. My mom left my birthday present in Mrs.

Washington's car so I couldn't find it early, since
I'll be at my dad's for my birthday on Saturday.
2. If the prank was messing up your hair at
Nevaeh's pool party, I heard about that already.
Jackson is my cousin. ~~He's kind of~~
3. Since our topic is jr. high friendships ending—
you obviously have firsthand data. An interview
with both of you for another article would be
good?

Rylee's stomach, already a tightened ball of dread
from even thinking about the pool party, did a sicken-
ing flip as she read the last sentence. She was already
shaking her head by the time she picked up her pen.
She wrote while Ms. Johnston passed stacks of fly-
ers for the play *To Kill a Mockingbird* down the aisle,
reminding them to have their parents sign the digital
permission form on the school site. Rylee glanced at
the flyer and kept writing. She had already seen the
movie, and this was *much* more important.

1. Happy Birthday Early! she wrote as quickly and
neatly as she could. 2. It was more than that. 3. I don't
~~want~~ think an interview is a good idea. ~~Aaliyah isn'~~ ~~I just~~
~~wanted you to know~~ Also: What did Jackson say?? He's
kind of what?

202

DeNia unfolded the note and scribbled a few lines. She crossed something out, frowning.

Ms. Johnston dismissed the class from homeroom, and DeNia dropped the note on Rylee's desk before picking up her backpack and joining the rest of the students leaving.

Rylee unfolded the paper and read DeNia's spiky handwriting as she merged into the outgoing tide of students.

1. Thank you!
2. Jackson was kind of surprised you got all huffy about your hair, TBH. He said you LEFT the whole PARTY. ~~I think he felt kind of bad about that.~~
3. Okay, I'll interview A.W., nbd.

No big deal.

Rylee rubbed her forehead as if hoping to dislodge DeNia's horrible idea from the folds of her brain. DeNia interviewing Aaliyah was just a great plan, obviously. Aaliyah would tell the truth, and explain why she and Nevaeh had been such jerks, and everything would be just peachy. Obviously.

16

Standoff

School was out, and around them people streamed from the eighth-grade wing in a hollering, shoving, laughing mass. Rylee and DeNia stood on the front walk like a little island in a wild sea of chaos, and DeNia was glaring at her.

"Look, Rylee, I don't get why you're upset. It's just a few questions, basically the same question from the survey that *you* wrote, which is 'what ended your last friendship?' I'll text you everything I'm going to ask her. She'll give us, like, a sentence or two, then boom—we've got another article. And I promise you, firsthand reporting like this is what gets you an A, you'll see."

"I'm just not comfortable because what happened last summer is . . . kind of personal."

"Rylee, it was *last. Summer.*" DeNia hefted her backpack with a loud sigh. "It's old news. Even if it feels like a big deal, I promise you it's not. People move on pretty quick."

Rylee shifted her weight uncomfortably. "I know, but—"

"Especially people in groups. They have a short attention span, like fruit flies. Did you know about that?" DeNia asked, suddenly in science mode. "It's not actually goldfish, like people think. Fruit flies have the shortest attention spans of anything in the animal kingdom. Actually, comparing us to animals might be kind of an interesting way to think about things like friends. Maybe we could compare people in groups to packs of wolves or something."

Fruit flies? Wolves!? Rylee would have laughed at the weird jumps DeNia's brain took, except she was too stressed. "Can't you write about wolves without talking to Aaliyah?"

A car came into the parking lot and DeNia peered at it, then glanced back at Rylee as she shifted her backpack and stepped off the sidewalk. "No—and I should go. My mom's picking me up and I have to be right there by the car pool stop when she gets there, or she gets all hyper."

At Rylee's expression, DeNia sighed. "Look, I promise I'll send you the questions before I send them to Aaliyah."

Rylee gripped the strap of her backpack. "DeNia, I just don't want anyone talking about what happened!"

"Nobody even cares about it anymore!" DeNia exclaimed. "No offense, Rylee, but come *on*. If I'm interviewing Aaliyah, and I'm not even putting your name on anything, can't you just—" At the curb, another car slid to a stop, and DeNia turned.

"Shoot—that's my mom," she said, and started running toward the front gate, giant backpack bouncing as she went. "I'll text you!"

Rylee wished nobody would ever say the words "no offense" ever again. They never meant what they promised: that no one would be offended. Rylee wasn't convinced "nobody even cares" wasn't the most offensive thing she'd ever heard. *She* cared. A lot.

DeNia probably would text her, but there wasn't any point. All that would happen is DeNia would think of another really good reason why Rylee should do what she wanted, and they would go round and round some more, and in the end, Rylee would feel like she did now, like she'd gotten run over by someone with a lot less panic swooshing around inside her, and a lot better arguments.

It was so blustery out that Rylee had been prepared to take the bus home, but she was churning too much inside to stand still and wait, so she started walking, stomping, really, the heels of her boots striking a sharp rhythm on the sidewalk.

Rylee wished she didn't care at all what Aaliyah might say in an interview about friendships ending. She wasn't going to tell the truth about what happened at Nevaeh's house, that was certain. Aaliyah was going to make up something that made her look good, and make it seem like Rylee had done something to deserve everything, and it would be—horrible. *I'm not even putting your name on anything,* DeNia had said, but that didn't mean no one would know that she was the ex-friend. The Spite Sisters would all know, and that was four people too many.

The wind swirled more leaves around Rylee's feet and sliced cold fingers through her sweater. She was just a block from home when the first sprinkle of rain spattered against her forehead.

"Oh, *great,*" she muttered, and started to run.

* * *

With his salt-and-pepper hair covered by a ball cap, Daddy Warren was trying to gather the last of the leaves as Rylee ran up the driveway. The wind flicked spatters of rain in all directions, and suddenly Rylee wanted to work hard and fast and throw herself at *doing* instead of thinking for once. Aggressively hunting down leaves sounded just perfect. She tossed her backpack on the porch swing and ran to help, kicking the golden, fan-shaped ginkgo leaves fluttering around the edges of the yard and regathering them into their pile.

Daddy Warren looked up with a grin and tugged his cap over Rylee's braids as she grabbed the rake to corral some leaf-pile escapees. "There's my girl. We'll have this done in no time now."

The work definitely went faster with two pairs of hands. Rylee used the rake to deposit her loads into the green waste can while Daddy Warren stuffed down armloads of leaves with his gloved hands. Rylee squeaked and grabbed for the lid as a heavy gust of wind threatened to topple the can and dump leaves everywhere. And then the clouds grew somehow heavier, and the spatters of rain increased to a torrent.

"Inside!" Daddy Warren called over the wind.

Handing back the cap, Rylee sprinted for the porch,

her cheeks tingling. She blew into the house and wiped her damp face, shivering as the warm air made her aware of just how cold her nose was. She wiped her feet on the mat and hurried up the stairs to change. She'd gotten wetter than she'd realized.

Once she'd changed her damp clothes for a fleecy sweatshirt and leggings, Rylee went down to the kitchen for a snack and found Daddy Warren leaning against the sink, warming his hands around a steaming cup. Geema was stirring something on the stove.

"Hey, Miss Rylee," Geema said, and pressed a kiss to her forehead as Rylee leaned against the counter next to her. Geema tsked. "Rylee, your face is freezing. Warren, get this child some coffee."

"You don't have to," Rylee said quickly. No matter how delicious it smelled, all the times Geema had given her a taste, coffee had been a disappointment as bitter as earwax. Geema liked hers "as black as midnight." At least Daddy Warren added milk.

"I've got it," Daddy Warren said, opening the refrigerator. He poured a thin stream of milk into one of the thick ceramic mugs that hung from hooks beneath the cupboards. When the milk covered the bottom of the mug, he added coffee from the machine, a giant, heaping spoonful of sugar, and, with a wink at

Rylee, another. Steam rose from the tan liquid as her grandfather set the coffee in front of her.

"Drink this down and you'll warm right up," he said, tweaking her ear.

"Thanks, Daddy Warren." Rylee took a tiny, bitter-milky sip and hid a grimace. Even the sugar didn't fix it. Since her grandparents thought they were giving her a treat, she would drink it . . . but *ugh*.

From Rylee's pocket came the chirp of her phone. That was probably DeNia, sharing the questions. Rylee sighed. She'd rather drink ten cups of terrible coffee than think about this interview.

With her phone a heavy weight in her pocket, Rylee let herself be nudged out of the way as Geema bustled around, starting the rice cooker, pulling things out of the freezer, and chopping onions. Rylee sat at the table and took microsips, listening to her mother and Geema taste-testing the soup and arguing about what else it needed. Geema wanted to add hot sauce.

None of the bustle distracted her for long from the phone burning a hole in her pocket.

Heaving a big sigh, Rylee finally looked at the text, and sure enough, it was a looong one with five questions, multiple choice, and answers to write out.

Think about friendships. Why did your last friendship end?

Ugh. Rylee turned her phone face down on the table and pinched the bridge of her nose. "Why?" was the question. It had never been about her bra size, or any questions Aaliyah or Nevaeh might have had. "Why?" was a question Aaliyah wouldn't answer.

Or maybe she'd simply answer, "Because." Because Aaliyah was absolutely *horrible.*

Geema turned down the soup to a simmer. "Well, my show's on," she announced, and left the room. Daddy Warren went out to the garage to look at Mom's brakes, and Rylee immediately shoved her cup of coffee across the table toward her mother, who laughed.

"I don't know why you don't just tell her you don't like coffee," her mother said, watching as Rylee dug into the refrigerator to find herself something to wash away the bitter taste.

"Because," Rylee said stubbornly, pouring herself a glass of chocolate milk.

"You've been awfully quiet sitting there. Is everything all right? School okay?"

"I'm all right. Just thinking," Rylee said, settling back at the table.

"Nothing wrong with that," Mom said, squeezing

her shoulder lightly. She took another sip of coffee and headed out of the room. "I'm upstairs if you need me."

"Thanks," Rylee said, finishing the milk.

She had just risen to rinse her glass when Axel came through the kitchen door, cold air and the smell of wet wool gusting behind him. He pushed off his hood and shrugged out of his coat.

"Hey," he said, leaving his backpack in the middle of the floor while he made a beeline to the cupboard to grab a glass. "If you want me to answer your question thing, I have something like fifteen minutes before we log on to Wizards."

Rylee had almost forgotten she'd put out the trash on Axel's day in return for his participation. "Really? You don't have to do homework first?"

"Nope." Axel popped the *p* smugly. "I finished at Jason's." Then he ruined his moment by tripping over his own backpack. Rylee yelped as chocolate milk sloshed in his glass—fortunately just onto his shirt and not on the floor. Unconcerned, Axel pulled the shirt into his mouth one-handed, and sucked off the liquid. With his other hand, he dragged a chair away from the table and sat down, face attentive. "Come on. Let's get this over with."

17

To Build a Bridge

It was just plain *weird* to sit with Axel when he wasn't being a goofball. After the shirt-sucking thing, he'd settled down to do the survey like . . . a normal person with something to say, not her slightly grungy, game-obsessed brother.

So weird.

"Okay, then, what makes a best friend? Or, maybe I should ask, *why* is Blake your best friend?"

Axel shrugged. "I dunno, he just is. His older brother was my book buddy in kindergarten, and we were tight after that. Plus, he had a stegosaurus, and I didn't."

Rylee snickered. "Right. So, he knew how to share, and that's why you liked him?"

"I guess," Axel shrugged again, scratching his elbow. "In kindergarten, Blake always had my back. He told me when Sawyer Hutchins took my triceratops." Axel paused a moment. "Sawyer is still kind of a jerk."

"I'm guessing the Ten Million Wizards game also has dinosaurs, huh?" Rylee asked, unable to stop her smile this time.

Axel gave her a look. "No. It has *dragons*. And I'm not doing this if you make fun of me, Rylee."

Rylee tucked her lips between her teeth. "Sorry. So, what do you do when you and your friends fight? I mean . . . you guys do fight, right? Sometimes I hear you yelling at your game."

"Yeah, sometimes," Axel admitted. "Sometimes one of us makes a dumb move during a campaign, and we get into it, or . . . you know, sometimes we get mad about stuff at school. Or sometimes somebody's just in a bad mood. Or—you know. People have stuff going on." Axel made a vague gesture. "Stuff people don't know about. Like, Sawyer's little sister already broke her gaming system once, and her stepmom's having another baby. Stuff like that."

"Huh," Rylee said, realizing she felt a little surprised that Axel would know so much about feelings—anyone's, really, but his understanding of his friends' feelings was especially surprising. He was always so . . . Axel-ish, it was hard to imagine.

"So, what do you do when you have a fight? Like, what if someone starts joking around, and goes too far with . . . maybe a prank or something?" Rylee asked. "Like, what do you do now if Sawyer is a jerk?"

"I tell her to knock it off," Axel shrugged.

Rylee studied her brother, somehow unable to imagine this. "So, you talk to her about it in front of your other friends, or when there's a problem, do you go talk privately or . . ."

"No, I tell everybody right then to knock it off," Axel said. "If people are being mean, you have to tell them. Sometimes, they really don't know," he explained earnestly. "Like Sawyer just . . . sometimes she's just messing around, but she gets all wound up and she says stuff she doesn't really mean. You have to tell her it bothers you, or she won't know that she should stop."

Rylee tried to imagine herself doing that while shivering and clutching a wet bathing suit. "What if they're being mean on purpose?" she asked.

"None of my *friends* are mean on purpose." Axel frowned. "Sometimes Sawyer is just messing around, or Blake's in a bad mood, or Marco or Jayse are mad about something else, but if they're mean to me on purpose, how are they supposed to be my friends?"

"Right," Rylee said hurriedly. Of course, that's what he thought. Friendships were easier in sixth grade. What did her brother know? He was only eleven. "Exactly. Okay, cool. Last question . . ."

Rylee asked her brother something about learning from ending friendships, but she was only halfway concentrating on what he was saying, glad to let the phone record his answer for later. If only Axel's world was the real one. If he was right—and he really couldn't be, could he?—she would have just said something when everything was happening. When people were being annoying, or hurtful, you *had* to tell them, after all.

There was no way it could be that easy.

"Make sure you put my name right on the article," her brother was saying.

"What?" Rylee scowled. "I know how to spell your name, boy."

"Axel is just for my friends, not for when I'm being

216

serious," Axel said. "Put Alexander Swanson, so people know I'm being real."

Now Rylee looked up, blinking. "Your whole name? Seriously? Not just 'Alex'?"

"Yep." Her brother tipped back his head and swigged the last of his milk and stood, his empty glass dangling loosely from one hand. "Are we done? Wizards is in about five minutes, and I need chips."

And there was her snack-scarfing, game-obsessed sibling back again. "Yeah, we're done. Thanks for answering my questions."

Rylee also stood—stepping over Axel's backpack, which she was pretty sure he was going to trip on again, probably carrying a sandwich the next time—and wandered up the stairs.

Geema had lined the stairwell with a gallery of photographs of Rylee and Axel at various ages with variously missing teeth and goofy-looking hair. In last year's picture, Axel had been caught with his mouth open, half laughing as if he was midword in one of his bad jokes. When Mom or Rylee weren't around, Axel seemed like he was always talking—to Blake, or Sawyer, or Marco, or any of his other gaming friends. He'd always been more outgoing than Rylee, had been invited to more kids' birthday parties, and been the louder, friendlier, center-of-attention kid to her quiet hanging-on-the-edges personality. Somehow all of that translated to him being much more confident in his friendships. Rylee wondered what would have happened if it had been Axel at the pool party. He would probably have wrapped the towel around his head and worn something of Nevaeh's like her long, red puffer coat or her fluffy bathrobe until she gave him back his clothes.

Why hadn't Rylee thought of something like that? Why hadn't she done something funny and outrageous instead of freaking out? Here it was, almost a whole four months later, and she was still having bad dreams about it. No wonder Mom called her "sensitive."

Rylee frowned and sat down on her bed. She pulled her phone out of her sweatshirt pocket and glared at its sparkly jeweled case. She couldn't do this. She couldn't pretend that Aaliyah was just someone she wasn't hanging out with anymore. Maybe Axel was right? Maybe, to get DeNia to stop pushing, she needed to tell DeNia what was *really* bothering her about it—and be sure she was listening.

Maybe that meant telling her the truth?

BOTH SIDES OF THE STORY:

Questions for the *Segrest Sentinel* Science Report

Think about friendships. Why did your last friendship end? How much responsibility do you share for your "friend-breakup"? Is it:

    a. 100% on you

    b. 50% on you

    c. 0% on you

    d. Some other amount _____

What's your friendship style? Are you:

    a. Outgoing, with a big circle of friends, and close with everyone

    b. Part of a big circle of friends, but with one or two close friends

    c. Part of a big group, but not really close with anyone

    d. Good to hang out by yourself or with one other person

Does what YOU believe ended your friendship match what your ex-friend thinks? Y/N

Finish this sentence: A friend is . . .

Scientific research shows that friendships in junior high don't last through high school. Do you agree or disagree? Why?

What is one thing that you know about friendship that can be applied to every student at Segrest / the whole world?

Late Friday night, Rylee was still undecided. She picked up her phone, then dropped it on the bedspread to wipe her sweaty palms. DeNia had texted her three times now, but Rylee just couldn't answer when she didn't know yet what to say.

It wasn't that there were that many questions, but they made Rylee tense just reading them. Was it 100 percent Aaliyah and Nevaeh's fault? Had Rylee done something? Maybe the whole thing had been Nevaeh's idea, so it was only 50 percent Aaliyah's fault? Who could even figure out blame like that?

And was there anything to "fix," really? What if Aaliyah thought there was? What if Aaliyah *tried* to make up with Rylee, after this? What was Rylee supposed to say?

Rylee curled up on herself like a defensive armadillo, wishing she had actual armor on. Did Aaliyah *really* not care anymore about what had happened? Would it matter to DeNia if she did care?

Rylee rubbed her face. She couldn't control what DeNia wrote, and maybe she was right—maybe the whole thing was over. They would turn in these articles, and not work together next time, and it would all be fine, right?

The phone chimed and Rylee tensed. DeNia. With a big sigh, she tapped to answer the Face2Face call.

"I was just going to text you," she told DeNia quickly.

"Finally! So you got the questions?" DeNia's face was slightly distorted by the camera.

"Yeah, sorry," Rylee said quickly. "Listen, DeNia—"

"You took forever, so I already sent them to Aaliyah," DeNia interrupted. "She'll get back to me with answers on Monday, and she's super excited to talk about friendship, which, she said, is her 'very favorite topic.' Leo is doing a poll about if guys have different kinds of friendships than girls—there was a psychology study about that. Anyway, it's done, okay? Sorry I didn't wait for you, but . . . I'd gotten kind of excited and mentioned it to Aaliyah at school anyway." DeNia winced. "It would be kind of ick if I didn't send her questions."

"That's . . . fine," Rylee said weakly, feeling her stomach plummet.

Well. That was that, then. It had happened just like she'd expected. DeNia had done what she was going to do anyway. This was their last article to turn in, and Rylee's last chance.

She took a deep breath and tried to let it go. "Well . . . it's been good working with you."

DeNia snorted out a laugh. "You don't need to say that, Rylee. I know you hated it."

"I'm serious," Rylee said, realizing it was true. "It wasn't . . . bad. It's kind of a trip working with someone so *into* everything, you know? I mean it," she added, as DeNia laughed again. "Your brain is *nothing* like mine, but you just kind of share whatever interesting thing you're thinking about, even if I don't know what you're talking about. And even though the Aaliyah part is kind of . . . a lot," Rylee admitted and blew out a sigh, "I'm glad I got to work with you. Even though I kept messing up."

"Um . . . okay. Thanks, I guess?" DeNia said with a hesitant smile. She looked awkward and sincere. "I know you don't believe me, but I really do think this is going to be a good article. People losing friends is part of friendship, and . . . that's what we're doing, so . . ."

"You're right, I guess." Rylee shrugged, and both girls sat silent for a moment.

Maybe it didn't matter anymore, keeping the secret of what had happened at Nevaeh's house. Aaliyah was going to . . . do Aaliyah, no matter what. She was probably spilling tea on her version of what happened, and nobody knew Rylee's truth. If she never opened her mouth, nobody *would* know.

Maybe the biggest truth was that Rylee was tired of holding on to everything by herself.

"Sometimes I feel like I don't know anything about it. Friendship, I mean. Losing friends, keeping friends. Who my actual friends are hasn't always been that clear," Rylee said.

DeNia's eyes widened. "Ohhh. So, you're saying Aaliyah . . . wasn't actually your friend?"

"*Hah*," Rylee said, but the noise she made wasn't a laugh. "Remember when I asked what Jackson had said about Nevaeh's party? I think Aaliyah and Nevaeh told him to cannonball me and went into the house. I got soaked and I was freezing, so, I went in, too, to change to dry clothes . . . but they were gone." Rylee swallowed, feeling the rough canvas of her bag beneath her fingers, her stomach swooping all over again as she cataloged its contents: her lotion, her deodorant, her wide-toothed comb, the once-favorite lip gloss that she hadn't worn since. The terrible suspicion that had pressed against her throat and crawled down into her stomach.

Rylee cleared her dry throat. "And then I heard the rest of my friends laughing in the closet."

"Wait, who was gone?" DeNia sounded confused. "They were in the closet? While you were getting dressed?" At Rylee's nod, DeNia's expression cleared, as she suddenly got the whole picture. "And where were your clothes?"

"Under Nevaeh's mattress," Rylee said.

"Ugh, that is . . . Some people are so immature." DeNia sounded disgusted.

Rylee continued. "I didn't realize they'd taken everything until I was already undressed, and then I didn't figure out they were *watching* . . ." Rylee shrugged. "It was kind of a disaster."

DeNia's expression was sad. "Rylee, I am so sorry that happened to you."

It was nice that DeNia was reacting sympathetically, that someone else thought what they'd done was as bad as she'd thought, but Rylee was done talking about it. "Yeah. So, *anyway*, they gave back my clothes . . . eventually." She made a face. "And then I went home."

DeNia's image loomed as she changed position, her light brown eyes seeming to peer through the camera into Rylee's face. "I don't . . . why would they do that, though? I thought you guys were tight."

Rylee shook her head, finding DeNia asking the same questions she'd asked herself. "I know, right? I ran into Cherise at the library a few weeks ago. She said Aaliyah wanted to know my bra size or something."

"Your bra size? When everybody has breasts, and they're just, literally, glands? That is the *most* bizarre thing I have heard today," DeNia said. "Jeez, I hate mean people! Nobody has the right to know things just because they want to know them. And they got my cousin all up in their nonsense? Yeah, that's not ever happening again. I'm going to tell Jackson—"

"Wait!" blurted Rylee. It felt so good to finally tell someone the truth. It had felt even better to have DeNia take her side, but in this moment, Rylee was remembering that once a secret was shared, it could be shared *again*. Now her heart was pounding so hard, she couldn't take a deep breath, and there were spots across her vision.

"DeNia, promise me you won't tell *anyone*. Please!"

18

Birds of a Feather . . .

"*Breathe!* **That's not** what I meant! That's not what I meant! *Rylee!*" DeNia's voice was tinny. "Are you still there? *Rylee!* Hello!?"

Rylee had dropped her phone from her sweaty hands, but now she picked it up, face hot with embarrassment. "I'm breathing," she said, and cleared her throat. "Sorry."

DeNia gave her a wary look. "Dang, girl—I didn't mean to freak you out. All I meant was I'm going to tell my cousin Jackson not to talk to Aaliyah and Nevaeh anymore. And Rosario and Cherise, too. I can't believe Cherise would do that. I thought she was pretty nice."

"Yeah . . ." Rylee sighed. She'd thought all her

friends were nice, mostly. "It's hard sometimes to be the one to stop things when they start, though."

"I guess," DeNia said. They sat in moody silence for a moment before DeNia sighed unhappily. "Okay, we need another article for the paper, then. Nathan is going to kill us, because I already talked to him about adding Aaliyah's article to the back page. We need something to fill the spot that was going to be for 'Both Sides of the Story.'" Since nobody needs to hear from Aaliyah, we have to find something else."

"Ohhhhh." Rylee felt her shoulders lower as stress poured out of her in a welcome rush. "Thank you, DeNia. But are you sure? I mean if she just talks about friendship, like you said . . ."

"Then we'll maybe save it for something else, but I'm not going to disrespect you like that, Rylee. We still need something to fill the spot, though." DeNia sighed.

"Um." Rylee drummed her fingers. "We could interview teachers about friendships?"

DeNia shook her head. "We will . . . but can we save them for later? We put in the article with your old people. We need Segrest students this time, people who like to see themselves in the paper, so they'll take our survey."

"Right, right," agreed Rylee. "Hey—maybe my brother? No . . . you said Segrest people. Ugh, DeNia, I can't think. . . ." Rylee rubbed her forehead. "Maybe Leo will know someone?"

"Maybe," DeNia said, frowning as she chewed her bottom lip.

"*Oh!*" Rylee sat straighter. "Do you know Devon Eastman?"

"N— Maybe?" DeNia looked toward the ceiling as she thought. "Yes! She did a salt-dough contour map of Florida for science fair when she was in sixth grade, right?"

Rylee burst out laughing. "Girl, I don't know, you're the one who remembers that kind of thing. Her nona lives in Florida, so maybe. Anyway, we've been friends for a long time, but we kind of took a break last year because *we* had a misunderstanding, and now we're friends again. I don't mind you interviewing me about that—Devon's cool."

"Excellent! Okay, whew." DeNia looked relieved. "Since it's online already, you'll just need to get Devon to—" DeNia broke off at a muffled voice. "What, Daddy? No, I'm on the phone." There was another pause, and then DeNia said, "It's Rylee. Swanson." A heavy sigh. "No, Daddy, you don't know Rylee."

Rylee bit back a laugh as DeNia rolled her eyes and turned the phone around. "Um, Rylee, this is my dad."

Rylee waved at the blurry figure too close to DeNia's phone. "Hi, DeNia's dad."

DeNia turned the camera back to herself and sighed. "Sorry, I have to go. I'm only here until Sunday, and my dad wants us to spend 'quality time' together for my birthday and stuff."

"Have the best, best, *best* birthday tomorrow," Rylee said. "Um, I'll talk to Devon and get something to you on Monday so we can make Nate happy and stuff."

"That'll be good. Um, listen," DeNia said quickly. "Thanks for . . . what you said. About working with me, I mean. I know I can be kind of all over the place, and we had a lot of . . . misunderstandings. But I'm, um, glad I got to work with you, too."

"Definitely," Rylee agreed. "This has been *much* easier to do with a friend."

DeNia just waved, but her small, pleased smile brightened her eyes.

The sun was a waterlogged disk through the thick clouds outside as Rylee poked through the kitchen cabinets for a snack the next morning. Mom had taken Axel to get shoes, and Geema couldn't stand the thought of someone being near a cash register without her, so had gone along. Rylee and Daddy Warren were on their own in the house until Mr. Winslow had come over with his glasses and his book of crossword puzzles. He and Daddy Warren were mostly talking through a "cowboy picture" in the den, as Geema called the old Westerns they liked.

The doorbell rang just as Rylee handed Mr. Winslow the bowl of popcorn she had made.

"I'll get it," Rylee said, hurrying forward even as her grandfather heaved himself up from his recliner.

"No, Miss Thing, *I've* got it." Daddy Warren gently scooted Rylee behind him as she reached for the doorknob.

Rylee was just getting ready to say something—Daddy Warren had Opinions about children answering the door, even when they were thirteen and not exactly babies anymore—but she gasped with excitement instead when she saw a familiar umbrella collapsing to reveal a friendly face.

"*Devon!*" she shrieked. "You're *here!*"

"Well, look what the cat dragged in," Daddy Warren teased, as Rylee flung her arms around her friend. "Where have you been keeping yourself? Haven't seen you in a month of Sundays. And who's this?"

Startled, Rylee peered around Devon and discovered a second person edging into the shelter of the porch. "Oh!" she said belatedly as the figure yanked a black beanie off a tangle of silky dark hair. "Oh, jeez. Uh, um, Cameron! That's right, you're Cameron! Hey!" Cameron's shoulders hunched at this loud greeting, and Rylee gentled her voice. "Sorry. Hi."

Devon turned and tugged her companion forward. "Mr. Swanson, this is our classmate, Cameron Franklin," she said. "Cam, this is Warren Swanson, Rylee's granddad."

Cameron, bundled in an oversize gray sweatshirt and jeans, muttered something no one could understand and edged behind Devon.

Daddy Warren smiled, seeming to accept that Cameron wasn't the chatty type. "Well, it's always nice to have young people stopping by," he said, stepping back and ushering them inside. "Rylee was just having a bite to eat."

"Yeah, come in the kitchen," Rylee invited, bouncing on her toes. "I was thinking about making hot chocolate or something. Or are you hungry?"

"The popcorn smells really good," Devon admitted.

"We have regular, or kettle corn, or we have chips, or we could make something else . . . ?" Rylee looked back at Cameron, who just shrugged speechlessly, turning a blotchy red.

"I'll eat whatever," Devon said.

"You know where everything is," Rylee said as Devon dumped her jacket on a kitchen chair and started for the popcorn.

Cameron hovered near the kitchen doorway. Rylee shot Devon a glance. "Um, you can sit down," she invited.

Cameron shrugged.

Rylee looked at Devon again, but Devon was busily unwrapping her popcorn.

Cameron had been in Rylee's homeroom last year, but even after weeks of sitting together in Wednesday Forum, all Rylee knew of Cameron was a series of giant hooded sweatshirts, beanies, and silence. Nevaeh had referred to Cameron as "Clam" so often last year that Rylee had barely remembered to call them "Cameron" just moments ago. Still, the fact remained that Cameron barely talked, didn't smile, and was basically not really there, at school. Rylee vaguely remembered Devon saying that Cameron was part of her game group, which had to mean words came out at least *sometimes*. But right now, Cameron was just . . . existing, and Devon was acting like nothing about that was weird.

So, this was Devon trusting her enough to bring over one of her new friends . . . which, okay, cool. Rylee hadn't expected company, especially someone she didn't know, but if Devon was hanging out with Cam now, then Cam was okay in Rylee's book. But . . . how was Rylee supposed to talk to someone who wouldn't talk back?

Rylee shot Cam another nervous smile and turned back to anxiously watching the microwave. Why had Devon brought Cameron *today*? Okay, so she and Devon weren't going to re-create their sixth-grade sleepovers-every-weekend days, but weren't the two of them supposed to be working on making up for the lost time in *their* friendship? Why would Devon drag along someone silent and practically more shellfish than person?

Stop. Hadn't the science study pointed to insults also being like slapping people? Rylee grimaced. She needed to get that "shellfish" thing out of her head right *yesterday*. While Aaliyah and the others would have laughed, would have cracked more jokes on that "Cameron Clam, Silent Sam" thing they had started last year, Rylee was slowly realizing that kind of thoughtless teasing truly *hurt* people, and she wasn't doing it again. Not anymore.

Now that she knew better, as Ms. Angelou had said, she was going to *do* better.

Once she figured out how to talk to Cameron, anyway.

Rylee fretted silently as Devon chattered away, asking if there was any grated parmesan for the popcorn. Rylee got her a grater and a chunk of Geema's fancy pecorino, and then decided that cheese was a good idea.

"I'm going to make grilled cheese," Rylee announced, opening the fridge. "Um . . . I'll make one my favorite way, cheddar with green apples, but I'll make a normal one, too, just in case anybody else wants some, okay, Cam?" Rylee cleared her throat and kept talking before Cameron's silence could answer her again. "So. What have you guys been doing today?"

Devon started the microwave. "We were working on some stuff for Mouse Guard but then Mrs. Limos came over. . . . Remember her?"

Rylee grinned. Devon couldn't stand the neighbor next door, who had liked to pinch her cheeks and tell her how to get a boyfriend, even when Devon was little. "Ooh, your favorite-ist person," she teased.

"Yeah, right. She wants to introduce me to her nephew. I decided that meant it was a perfect day to see if you had time to show me your ukulele."

"Oh! Sure." Rylee straightened, suddenly realizing she had an even better way to make the awkward silences stop. "Actually, though, since I already have you here . . . um, and you, too, Cameron, can I get you to fill out a survey first?"

"A survey?"

"Weird."

Rylee straightened from where she was leaning against the pillow propped against her bedroom door. "What?" Had Cameron actually *said* something?

Cameron shrugged, and Rylee mentally shrugged back. *Okay, then.*

"Right, so the second question . . ."

"No, this is *really* weird," Cam interrupted in a voice husky from disuse. "Who thinks they can tell people what to wear? Who does that?"

Rylee sputtered. Now that Cameron was actually speaking to her, she felt awkward and self-conscious. "Well, um . . ."

Devon snorted and propped her heels on Rylee's headboard. "Remember Reina? Cam, get this—when we were in fourth grade, this one girl made all her friends wear only the colors she wore, every day."

"That's little kids, though," Cameron dismissed.

236

"Nobody actually *does* that!"

"*Bzzzt!* Wrong answer," said Rylee, making an obnoxious buzzer sound. "In sixth we made these lacy denim cutoffs, and last year Aaliyah decided we should get these lace platform high-tops, but we weren't supposed to wear them except when we wore the shorts, and—" Rylee broke off abruptly, realizing awkwardly that she was talking to Devon about Aaliyah, the person Rylee had ruined their friendship over.

"That sounds *really* stupid," Devon muttered, then looked up, chagrined. "Sorry, Rylee."

Rylee shrugged. "It's true. At first it was kind of fun to wear the same thing, you know, just to be . . . like, together. But it got old pretty fast to have to so many rules about it."

"Like I said, nobody *normal* or whatever actually does that," Cameron repeated after a moment's pause. With a challenging glance at Rylee, Cameron added, "You know she's kind of mean, right? Aaliyah told some girl in the bathroom last Wednesday that her haircut made her nose look 'sooo much smaller.' And then she left, and this poor girl is just, like—staring at herself in the mirror."

"Yeah, but that's just Aaliyah. You should hear what she said about the shirt I picked up from Thrift

Station." Devon raised her voice an octave to adopt Aaliyah's sugary-sweet tone. "Heeeeey, Dev, that shirt looks like it was made for you!"

Rylee was lost. "And that's . . . not good?"

Devon's lips twitched. "It's a bowling shirt," she said. "It has 'Sean' stitched above the pocket, and it's four sizes too big."

At Rylee's expression, Devon pretty much fell over laughing.

Cameron gave a long-suffering sigh and threw a piece of popcorn at Devon's head. "It's still not actually funny, Eastman."

"It kind of is, though." Devon snickered. "Whenever I laugh at Aaliyah, it weirds her out so hard! She likes it better when she thinks she hurt my feelings."

"Does she . . . try and hurt you? I mean, she says stuff like that to you all the time?" Rylee had known Aaliyah sometimes chose people to pick on—and she'd made a point of rolling her eyes at Devon's camouflage gear, but . . . had she kept *going*, after Devon hadn't even hung around with them anymore?

"Well, yeah, pretty much," Devon said, and added, at Rylee's disbelieving look, "I mean, she was doing it all of last year, at least. She's just *like* that, Rylee."

"Oh." Rylee's mind was too full of *everything* to say

anything. Had she actually not known how bad Aaliyah really was? How had she not paid attention to how Aaliyah treated other people?

"So, what's the next one?" Devon asked, rolling over to her side to peer at Rylee.

"What?" asked Rylee faintly.

"Next question?" Cam prodded. "Let's finish this."

They finished the survey, finally, with a bit more grumbling from Cameron at what they considered weird questions. Once everyone stopped throwing it, they even finished the popcorn. Cameron finally ate a Granny Smith grilled cheese sandwich and pronounced it good. Devon had a comic book from the Mouse Guard game stashed in a roomy pocket, and Rylee got her first look at what the game was about. They pulled up more of the playable characters on Rylee's laptop, and Cameron and Devon took turns explaining the world-building, and what the game objectives were. In the middle of Cameron reenacting a sword fight, a quiet knock interrupted.

"Hey, folks." Mom poked her head around the door with a smile. "Just wanted to know if I should thaw an extra loaf of sourdough for dinner or what. Geema made spaghetti."

Cameron, who had sucked in a startled breath when

239

the door opened, started coughing.

Devon sat up and thumped Cameron's back. "Oh, my gosh, it's almost *dark*. I hate how early it gets dark in October," she complained. "Thanks, Ms. Swanson, but I should go. Mom was starting something big roasting when I left, and Mrs. Limos probably went back to her house by now."

"Cameron, do you want some water?" Rylee asked, beginning to worry as Cameron's throat clearing continued.

With a silent head shake, Cameron mumbled something about going home.

And just like that, everyone was grabbing shoes and bags. The party was over.

Rylee shook stray popcorn pieces out of her hair as she walked her guests to the door.

"This was *fun*," Devon said fondly, and flung her arms around Rylee for a quick squeeze. "I'm so glad you were home."

"I would have *come* home if I wasn't," Rylee said, hugging her back. "Let's do this again."

Rylee turned to Cameron, whose beanie hat was back. All Rylee could see now beneath the blue yarn was a watchful pair of dark eyes. Cameron didn't look like a hugger.

"Um, so . . . thanks for coming, Cameron," Rylee said politely.

Too politely, it seemed, because Cameron kind of . . . snickered. "Yeah, this was all right. It was actually nice to meet you. I mean, you're . . . really not like I thought one of Aaliyah's friends would be."

Rylee's mouth opened, but she struggled a moment to find words through the emotion. "I'm not Aaliyah's friend," she said finally.

"Yeah, okay," Cameron shrugged. "You know what I mean, though."

"Is it still raining out there? Devon, why don't you all go get in the car." Daddy Warren bustled up, frowning out with concern at the dark, wet evening. "I'll run you all home right quick."

"Oh, Mr. Swanson, it's not that far!" Devon protested, but in the end, there was no arguing with him. And finally, there was another flurry of waving and hugs from Rylee, this time around the corner at Devon's house, where Cam insisted on getting out, too.

As Daddy Warren turned the car toward home, Rylee thought again about Aaliyah and Nevaeh, and how mean Aaliyah had been to Devon. She wondered again why it had never occurred to her that people might think she was just like them.

19

Two-Sided Story

The house had quieted for the night, but Rylee could still hear her mother's voice murmuring across the hall as she read aloud to Axel, who was probably going to get up and turn on his computer game again as soon as Mom finished the chapter.

The rain dripped from the eaves next to her window in a steady rhythm as Rylee wrapped her braids in a silk scarf and wriggled into her knee-length sleep shirt. She'd planned to read a little while herself, but her brain was still spinning, working through the things that had happened that day. She sat cross-legged on her bed with the quilling stylus and twisted strips of construction paper from the shredder into neat little coils instead.

This weekend had been all over the place. Rylee had been super nervous, then super happy, her emotions like a roller coaster. The way DeNia had reacted to hearing about Aaliyah when Rylee had finally told her everything still lay like a tiny ember in her chest, warming her from the inside, making everything better. That DeNia had immediately decided not to run the story—even though that had left her missing one of her three articles—told Rylee something important, that DeNia was a real friend, the kind that Rylee would want around for a long time.

And then there was Devon. Rylee shook her head in amazement. Devon was exactly the same as she'd been two years ago: kind, funny, and easy to just hang out with. Devon made dopey jokes, and laughed at them, she found everything everyone else said interesting, she asked good questions, and when her friends talked to her, she really listened, and gave them her attention.

Rylee had missed that. She hadn't noticed when her time with friends had turned stressful, and she'd felt like she'd had to be careful, to say things that wouldn't tick anyone off, to wear the right things, to laugh at the right times, and know about the right looks, and music, and shows. With Devon, Rylee hadn't realized how little she'd been judged all the time for every-thing, until she had been with a group of girls who did judge her, sometimes laughing at her for liking or saying or doing the "wrong" thing.

And even though Devon had brought Cameron over, even that had turned out to be more than just okay. Once Cam got comfortable, funny observations and good company followed. Rylee was slowly begin-ning to understand how much being around Nevaeh and Aaliyah had affected her ability to meet new peo-ple. She'd closed herself off to new friends, judging them from a distance. If Devon hadn't brought Cam over, maybe Rylee might have always simply thought of Cam as just a silent clam, instead of someone observant, detail oriented, and creative. Even though Mouse Guard sounded a little complicated for her tastes, Rylee thought she and Cameron might really be good friends, once they got to know each other a little better.

Rylee's fingers stilled on the quilling stylus. Cam's little comment about it being actually nice to meet her, because she wasn't what Cam had expected, still echoed in Rylee's brain. Even in the times when

Aaliyah had snapped at Rosario, or Nevaeh had made fun of Cherise, it had never occurred to Rylee that even *they* might have thought she approved of the way those girls acted. She had been angry because no one had defended her . . . but had she ever stuck up for *them?*

And then, Aaliyah still hassling Devon? Somehow, that was the worst, since Devon wasn't some imaginary person Aaliyah could give a dumb nickname to and make jokes about. They had all three been friends, once, Rylee had thought. But it was clear now that the more she *thought* she knew about friendship, the less she actually knew at all.

Sighing, Rylee tucked the quilled paper into the plastic box with the rest and put her glue and stylus away. She was going to have to think about this some more. She felt suddenly protective of her friendships, all of them so new and fragile. Rylee wasn't going to put up with Aaliyah or anyone trying to wreck things.

Not anymore.

This time, Rylee was prepared for the weather. Wearing her see-through raincoat and stompy leopard-print rain boots—a gift from Geema last year—she splished to the bus stop on Monday morning to catch the early bus, full of determination. Daddy Warren had fussed at her for refusing a ride in the car, but the bus today was a good idea. It helped Rylee's busy brain to have more things to think about.

For instance, Rylee had to think about how she kept her hood tilted, to keep the rain off her face. She had to think about how close she stood to the curb, so the passing cars didn't send sprays of dirty water onto her jeans. She had to think about how many stops until the one before school, where she got out and walked across the parking lot and to her classroom.

It helped a lot to have something to think about other than the fact that DeNia had texted **BEFORE SCHOOL, talk tomorrow** to her Sunday night, and then not texted back, even though Rylee had sent **What's up** and **Why?** and **What's going on?????** replies, like, six times.

After everything they'd talked about on Friday, this gave Rylee a *really* bad feeling. But . . .

Fact: DeNia was honest—and even if she had something bad to tell Rylee, she'd say it.

Evidence: When DeNia was still mad at Rylee, she'd just stopped talking instead of lying about how she felt.

Reasoning: Even if something really bad was wrong, DeNia would tell the truth, and Rylee could work with that.

This wasn't going to be that bad . . . right?

Already fast-walking, Rylee got an extra shove through the doors from the wind, and then she was swimming upstream with a few of her classmates, crossing squeaky linoleum floors while shedding her plastic raincoat. She headed toward Ms. Johnston's classroom.

"Rylee! Over here!"

DeNia was waving to her from the drinking fountain, wrapped in an oversize gray raincoat and wearing a cute headband scarf. Her teeth were pressing her bottom lip firmly, giving her the appearance of a slightly worried squirrel.

"What?" Rylee burst out, scanning DeNia's face. "Are you okay? What happened!?"

DeNia's widened eyes told their own story. "So *much* is happening—but first . . . well, I got here early because I needed to talk to Nate about Aaliyah's article, but—look at this. Look!"

Rylee took the paper DeNia thrust into her hand and recognized Aaliyah's handwriting.

BOTH SIDES OF THE STORY:

Questions for the *Segrest Sentinel* Science Report

Think about friendships. Why did your last friendship end? How much responsibility do you share for your "friend-breakup"?

Is it:

    a. 100% on you I chose to move on.

    b. 50% on you

    c. 0% on you

    d. Some other amount _____

What's your friendship style? Are you:

    a. Outgoing, with a big circle of friends, and close with everyone Yay besties!

    b. Part of a big circle of friends, but with one or two close friends

    c. Part of a big group, but not really close with anyone

    d. Good to hang out by yourself or with one other person

Does what YOU believe ended your friendship match what your ex-friend thinks? Y N

Finish this sentence: A friend is . . .

Someone completely on Team Aaliyah who is really not about DRAMA! They always have my back, know how to make me laugh and have fun, like the same things that I like, and can TAKE A JOKE, which is super important!!

Scientific research shows that friendships in junior high don't last through high school. Do you agree or disagree? Why?

I agree that friendships probably don't last forever in school—because not everyone can rise to the same level. YKWIM, some people are really too immature to really hang out with on the level that you can other people. Some people change too much to be cool with their old friends. Some people are only meant to be the kinds of friends that you eat lunch with, or whatever, and it doesn't work to do other stuff. Some friends you hang out with in a class or something, and then you go to the next class, no biggie. Not everybody is built to be your ride or die forever friend. That's too much pressure, right!? People

should be cool with friends just coming and
going, that's what I think.

I've had friends who were pretty chill or
whatever, but this year, we don't hang. Which,
whatever, you know? Not everybody goes the
distance. Stay tight with your friends who
do, and don't stress about the rest.

**What is one thing that you know about friendship
that can be applied to every student at Segrest / the
whole world?**
    Everybody needs friends like mine!

Rylee read, and then reread Aaliyah's answers
again . . . and again, exhaling out all the conflicting
feelings swirling through her. Aaliyah had moved *on*!?
She thought people couldn't come to her *level*!? She
was joking, right? Did Aaliyah really think she was
that . . . awesome? She could be annoying sometimes,
yeah, but Rylee couldn't believe anyone was seriously
that . . . ridiculous. Sure, everyone should believe in
themselves—it was what created self-esteem. But people had to be honest with themselves, too, deep down
when no one was looking. Aaliyah was totally lying in

this survey, even, it seemed, to herself.

Finally, when she felt steadier, Rylee looked up at DeNia. "You know, Nate would fully *murder us* if we ever turned in something like this."

DeNia's laugh was way louder than Rylee's comment deserved. "Rylee!"

"Well, he would," Rylee said, handing the paper back and turning to walk the rest of the way to homeroom. "Did you hear him tell Leo to delete all the 'ands' and 'thes' from his article so his eyeballs would stop bleeding? Aaliyah's writing would give him some kind of heart attack."

DeNia fell into step with Rylee, sighing. "Oh, whew. I thought you'd be upset."

Rylee scoffed, her bitter feelings seeping into the sound. "Why, though? She didn't write about me! Aaliyah wrote about Aaliyah—because Aaliyah's all about Aaliyah, twenty-four seven. I don't know why I expected anything else."

"So, true, right?" DeNia turned to walk backward, folding her hands beneath her chin, and giving Rylee her best pleading face. "Soooo, Rylee . . . ? If you're not mad, though, and this isn't about you . . . would you maybe *think* about me maybe running this in the paper?"

Rylee rolled her eyes. "Stop making puppy eyes. It's fine."

DeNia batted her eyes and looked even more pleading. "Cool, but . . . would you also maybe, maybe, please think about writing something, too? *Please?*"

Rylee stopped walking. "Wait. Something like what?" she asked, a frown hovering.

"Nothing personal like, about you, or what happened," DeNia said firmly, straightening to speak more seriously. "Just, maybe you could write a paragraph about, like . . . how it is to be . . . not Aaliyah? Like, how to figure out where to be and stuff if you're not with your old friends anymore? I thought somebody should write about the library at lunch and stuff—I mean, it might be cool for a student to say, instead of teachers making announcements at homeroom every time."

"I . . . guess," Rylee said slowly, thinking it through. It would have been good to be reminded about the library, right at the beginning of school. She'd been lucky to stumble on Leo giving her his library pass, lucky Mom had given her so many good suggestions, even when she hadn't been ready to listen to them.

"I could write something, yeah," Rylee said, giving DeNia a firm nod, deciding she wouldn't feel so unsure once she got started. "I mean, if Aaliyah can put her ideas out there, I kind of *have* to put out mine, right?"

"Great, great, cool," DeNia said, still seeming a little nervous for some reason. "And, you can get that to me by the end of journalism, too, right?"

Rylee's mouth dropped. "Wait, *what?* You want this for the back page of *this* issue? And, I'd have to turn it in to Scary Nate when it's almost late and he's going to yell at me!?"

"I know! I know! That's why I wanted you to come early!" DeNia blurted.

"How am I supposed to write an article in four periods!?" wailed Rylee. "I actually have to pay attention in language arts, *and* we have a geometry test!"

DeNia winced. "I know. I swear, I'll pay you back—I'll even take this to Nate, and he can yell at me because Aaliyah's stuff is going to need so much editing. But it's going to be so good this way! Aaliyah's article, and then yours, right next to it." DeNia gestured theatrically.

Rylee rolled her eyes.

"Oh, come on," DeNia begged. "You'll sit down and blow through the whole thing during Press Club at lunch, and I'll proofread it for you. You're a good writer, Rylee, and this is going to be *so* good, I swear."

"Ugh, I hate everything about this," grumped Rylee, but she didn't say no.

"Thank you, thank you, thaaaaank you," DeNia cheered, clapping her hands. "When we see our bylines, this is all going to be worth it."

The *Segrest Sentinel* Reports

SEGREST STANDPOINTS: Facts on Friendship
by DeNia Alonso & Rylee Swanson

***

The views and opinions expressed in the Segrest Sentinel are those of the students and do not necessarily reflect the official policies or positions of Segrest School. Survey responses may have been edited for length or clarity.

***

D E V O N • E A S T M A N

Q: What's your friendship style?

A: *I have a big circle of friends—but I tend to hang out with them in small groups when we're all doing our own thing, unless it's a game day.*

Q: Finish this sentence: A friend is . . .

A: *Someone who likes me and respects me and someone I can trust to be who they are, and to let me be me.*

Q: Scientific research shows that friendships in junior high don't last through high school. Do you agree, or disagree? Why?

A: *I don't know—I would have said I agreed a little while ago, because people change too much to be friends, BUT, one of my best friends and I just started hanging out again after basically not talking for a year. So, maybe friendships can last through junior high, because even though we change a lot, we sometimes maybe change back, too? I mean, it's possible, right?*

Q: What is one thing that you know about friendship that can be applied to every student at Segrest / the whole world?

A: *Talking to your friends about what matters to you makes it 100 percent easier to stay friends.*

N E V A E H • G R E E N

Q: What's your friendship style?

A: *I'm all about QUALITY, not quantity. I'm*

tight with just one or two people. People
don't need as many friends as they think
they do.

Q: **Finish this sentence: A friend is . . .**
A: *LOYAL. People come and go, but a real*
friend is loyal. They don't get in your
way if you're on your way up. They know
that you have goals and dreams, and they
step back when you're doing your thing.
(That's more than a sentence, but you can't
define friendship in just one.)

Q: **Scientific research shows that**
friendships in junior high don't last
through high school. Do you agree, or
disagree? Why?
A: *Agree—because people get too involved*
in their own drama, and they drop out.
Which is NBD—no big deal. Like I said,
you don't need that many people. All you
need is the ones who can seriously make an
effort to show up and make time for you.
Not everyone knows how, and that's not
something I can teach you. Maybe we learn

how to be there for our friends when we've had friends be there for us.

Q: What is one thing that you know about friendship that can be applied to every student at Segrest / the whole world?
A: *There's no such thing as losing a friend—there's only finding out who your real ones are.*

L E O • R I E S E N

Q: What's your friendship style?
A: *I'm pretty much friends with everyone, I guess. Maybe not all, but most.*

Q: Finish this sentence: A friend is . . .
A: *Somebody who has the same kind of interests and is easy to hang out with.*

Q: Scientific research shows that friendships in junior high don't last through high school. Do you agree, or disagree? Why?
A: *Probably agree? I'm still friends with everyone, but if it's just casual, like a*

friend you see in class, those friendships
change when your schedule changes. I guess
we'll see next year.

Q: What is one thing that you know about
friendship that can be applied to every
student at Segrest / the whole world?
A: *Friendship doesn't have a gender, a*
color, or an age. Deal with it.

A A L I Y A H • W A S H I N G T O N
Q: What's your friendship style?
A: *I have a big circle of friends, and I'm*
friendly with everyone.

Q: Finish this sentence: A friend is . . .
A: *Someone completely on Team Aaliyah, who*
is not about the drama, and who can take
a joke, which is super important.

Q: Scientific research shows that
friendships in junior high don't last
through high school. Do you agree, or
disagree? Why?
A: *I agree that friendships probably*

don't last forever in school—because not
everyone can rise to the same level. Not
everybody is built to be your ride-or-
die forever friend. People should be cool
with friends just coming and going. Not
everybody goes the distance.

**Q: What is one thing that you know about
friendship that can be applied to every
student at Segrest / the whole world?**
A: *Everybody needs friends like mine!*

20

Wolf-Pack Attack

Even though she'd hated reading DeNia's interview with Aaliyah, Rylee was still happy to collect compliments about their other friendship pieces. Students acknowledged her in homeroom, and in the halls between classes they'd smile or say she'd done a good job. It was both amazing and also kind of overwhelming. For someone who hadn't even *wanted* to join Press Club or take Journalism II, it was hard to know how to feel when even Principal Loughran-Smith winked at her and said, "Nice writing, Rylee Swanson. Keep it up."

To be honest, it was also kind of worrying that the principal knew who she was by sight.

And at home, the celebration had started even earlier. Mom had brought home a silver helium balloon that said Congratulations! and tied it to Rylee's chair at dinner. Geema served her triple lemon cake for dessert to celebrate Rylee's first time in print.

"I saved the whole newspaper for my scrapbook," Geema said proudly. "And when you win the Pulitzer Prize for writing someday, I'm going to pull it out and remind folks they knew you when."

"Aw, thanks, Geema," Rylee said, giddy with happiness and sugar. She couldn't imagine winning anything, but if all writing prizes came with lemon cake baked with lemon zest and drizzled with lemon juice syrup, she would write something every day.

"Hey, Geema? You know, I *helped* Rylee write that article," Axel said hopefully, trying to mold his greedy expression into puppy-like cuteness. "Does that mean I get another piece?"

Rylee snorted. Leave it to Axel to try and take some of the spotlight. "Get over yourself, goofball. I interviewed Geema, too. Daddy Warren *and* Mom also 'helped' me write my article, so you're not special."

Daddy Warren pulled the cake plate toward himself with a contented expression. "Well, that's all true," he said. "Seems to me if any of us are helpful like that, we should all have another piece."

"May as well cut me one, too," Geema said, trying to sigh like she was mad about it.

"I just want a little more frosting," Mom added, swiping a little of the powdered sugar and lemon glaze from the edge of her plate.

"I'll eat your piece, then," Rylee teased.

Even better than all the compliments, the following Wednesday during journalism, Ms. Johnston told the class that there were a few pieces in that first issue that might be good enough to qualify for their state's Junior High Press Awards.

"It's early to choose an issue of the paper to submit, of course, but the articles I see my reporters writing this quarter are the kinds of pieces I think the judges are looking for," Ms. Johnston said with a lift of her arched eyebrows.

This was especially exciting since Ms. Johnston had *been* one of the judges the year before.

But, the thing about newspapers was that they just kept going. Even though the *Sentinel* staff had only put out the monthly paper ten days earlier, there wasn't time to sit around and be proud of themselves. For the next edition, Rylee was researching a human-interest story about an opossum den some sixth graders had found in the wooded area by the canal near the back of the school property. The sixth graders wanted the opossums to be the Segrest School mascot. The school district wanted the county to relocate them. DeNia was working with Leo on a follow-up to his report about the school district's Universal Meals Program, which provided breakfasts and lunches over the summer for any student.

Rylee stepped out of the bathroom stall after study hall on Thursday, still mulling over the whole opossum thing, when she met the eyes of Rosario Torres, standing by the sink applying a shiny pinkish lip gloss.

"Hey," Rosario said, as if she'd just been hanging out, waiting for Rylee to appear. "Didn't know you were on the paper."

"Uh, yeah. Hi," Rylee said uncertainly. She washed her hands, wishing she wouldn't keep running into former friends in the bathroom.

Of all the Spite Sisters, Rylee found Rosario the hardest to read. She was tall and confident like Aaliyah and had the ability to mimic the voices and mannerisms of all the teachers, which would make Rylee laugh till she couldn't breathe. Even though she was funny, Rosario could also be really quiet, just kind of hanging out, saying nothing for hours. She'd been a good person to do homework with. Even when Nevaeh teased her about how big her curly hair was, or Aaliyah lectured her about learning Spanish "because you really should represent your people, Ro," she never acted like she was bothered, one way or another. She was the most chill person Rylee had ever met. Rylee had actually missed her, in a way.

"So, um—" Rylee was fumbling her way toward asking how things were going when another stall burst open, and everything went downhill.

"Oh, look, everyone, it's Rylee Writer," Nevaeh said loudly.

Rylee jumped, her hand flying to her throat. Beneath her fingertips, her pulse was pounding in her neck, and the tortilla soup she'd had with lunch burbled unhappily in her stomach. Ugh, why hadn't she remembered that the Spite Sisters traveled in packs? Aaliyah tended to keep talking to people from her bathroom stall, and Nevaeh always needed an audience for everything from flossing her teeth after lunch to standing in the hall making fun of her latest nickname victim. Rylee should have *known* seeing Rosario by herself was too good to be true.

"So, Rylee Writer, what's up?" Nevaeh continued her obnoxiously loud faux-friendly conversation as Rylee quickly dried her hands and tightened the high ponytail that held today's waterfall of pink-and-blonde box braids. "Aaliyah says that girl from the paper interviewed her? Are you going to interview anyone? I mean, anyone *interesting*—you know, not, like, old people or whatever? Because I filled out that survey thing."

Rylee grimaced inwardly. Nevaeh thought the article was boring, message received. "Cool," she said, and stepped around Nevaeh—who hadn't even started to wash her hands yet, *eww*—and headed toward the door. "Thanks for filling out the survey."

"Don't you want another interview?" Nevaeh asked.

Rylee turned, eyes widening. "*You* want me to interview you? For the Friendship Study?"

"Uh, *yeah*," Nevaeh said, as if it was obvious. "You know I have a lot of friends, and I have a lot more to say."

"Uh, great," Rylee fumbled, suddenly unable to even pretend that Nevaeh wasn't totally unnerving her. She hitched her backpack higher on her back, feeling sweat collecting in her armpits. "Yeah, so, the interviews were just kind of to introduce the study. The survey is mostly about friendships ending, and the rest of the reports are going to cover the school as a group—"

"If people decide they don't want to be friends any-more, it's NBD, you know? Because people come and go, but real friends *stay loyal*," Nevaeh said forcefully. "I have a lot to say about that, too. Some people think they can just walk away, but that's not how it works."

Rylee's fingers were strangling the backpack strap over her shoulder now. "Yeah. Got it," she said, then speed-walked to Mrs. LaPointe's class for social studies, trying to pretend she wasn't feeling shaky.

Today was *officially* the most unnecessary day of the week. Rylee wished she had risked going to the bathroom in the library, even though that might have made her late. Nevaeh's little lecture had made the message clear. "People" didn't need as many friends as they thought they did, and Rylee was one of the extras that people didn't need. Furthermore, she hadn't been a "real" friend. She hadn't been "loyal" because she'd walked away. Not even Rosario's wince of sympathy as Rylee had hurried out of the bathroom made her feel better.

She's just a mean person being mean, so don't cry about it, Rylee ordered herself, but that didn't stop her eyes from stinging. It wasn't even Nevaeh, really; her and Aaliyah's answers to the friendship survey had basically been about the same, and their ridiculous attitude of "we're so awesome" wasn't what gave Rylee a sick feeling in her stomach. It was, surprisingly, Rosario—Rosario, whom Rylee wished she could have gotten to know better. Rosario, whom Rylee had hoped she could still be friends with somehow, without Aaliyah or Nevaeh noticing. Rosario, who had just stood there, waiting, not saying a word as Nevaeh smirked and sniped and insulted Rylee.

Once upon a time, Rylee had been just like Rosario. How many times had she just stood there, and winced as someone else was the target of one of Nevaeh's mean little rants? How many times had she wished she could be anywhere else—but hadn't walked away?

Rylee opened her social studies book to the correct page and tried to pay attention to some facts about the effect of the American Revolution on France, but she couldn't stop the questions from spinning around in her mind. What would have happened to her if the pool party *hadn't* happened? Would she have continued to stand around through Nevaeh's snide remarks, or Aaliyah's sarcastic compliments to people? Would she have kept listening for gossip to share with Cherise or used another of the silly nicknames they'd thought of for everyone? Would Rylee have continued to ignore all the stuff that made her uncomfortable about her friends, and only focus on the fun they'd had together?

Rylee didn't know, and not knowing made the sick feeling in her stomach worse.

Ugh, she didn't want to think about this anymore. Rylee leaned her forehead in her hand and exhaled a long sigh, wishing that Thursdays were early-dismissal days.

The *Segrest Sentinel* Reports

Advice Column: Dear Uncle Leo
by Leo Riesen

Dear Uncle Leo: My best friend keeps blowing me off, and it's starting to get on my nerves. Last time I texted them, they didn't text me back until an hour later. Should I say something?

Fed Up in Friendstown

Dear Fed Up,

If you want to say something to your friend about what *they're* doing, make sure you're ready to hear what they have to say about you.

When someone doesn't spend as much time with you, and is busy when you want to do something, that might mean your time of being close friends is ending. People change a lot physically, mentally, and socially in junior high, and our friendships change, too. Saying something to your friend might help make it clear what's

270

going on, and help you make your next move.

Good luck!
Uncle Leo

Dear Uncle Leo: The boy I like won't talk to me, like, at all. He sits next to me in homeroom, but he's so shy I can barely get him to say more than "hi." Since you're a boy, can you tell me what a girl can do to make a boy talk to her?

The Girl with the Curls

Dear the Girl with the Curls,

You might not know this, but nobody can make anybody else like them. Not even if you're good-looking, or rich, or bring fudge brownies for lunch every day and share. If someone doesn't like you, they don't like you. Only *they* can change that.

This is true for anyone of any gender: if you're friendly to someone, and they're not

super friendly back, that's usually a sign
that they don't want to be friends. Your
next move is to find someone else to talk
to and leave them alone.

I know that's probably not what you want
to hear, but it's the truth.

Good luck,
Uncle Leo

The *Segrest Sentinel* Reports

Standpoints Sidebar: Some Friends REALLY Share . . . Everything!

by DeNia Alonso

***

As part of the activities of Press Club, this year eighth graders DeNia Alonso and Rylee Swanson are conducting a scientific journalism project about friendship. Throughout the semester, they will be reporting on different aspects of friendship and how it affects those of us in junior high.

***

From the information that has come in (thank you to everyone who has already filled out a Friendship Survey), your *Sentinel* reporters are seeing something we expected—a lot of similar answers to our survey. There could be a lot of reasons for that—most of the people who responded so far are of the same school, the same state, and the same grade. Some of them are taking the survey with friends, so their answers might even be identical. But another reason for these similarities is that good friends sometimes share *brain waves*.

We're not kidding! In 2018, a study was published in the journal *Nature Communications*. Dr. Carolyn Parkinson of the University of California, Los Angeles, and her partners hooked up scanners called functional magnetic resonance imaging (fMRI) to forty-two graduate students' brains. Then the students watched video clips of cute things, like baby sloths, or pictures of the Earth from space. Before they started watching the clips, the entire graduate school class filled out a survey and identified which of the other students in the group they considered to be their friend, and how close of friends they were.

It turned out, the brain patterns of friends were "exceptionally similar," and showed a pattern of people becoming friends who were the least different from each other. And the closer the friends, the more closely their brain activity was mirrored. Seeing the study results, researchers were even able to guess which of their subjects were friends without looking at their survey information—and they were right (Parkinson et al.).

Does this study mean that we only make friends with people who are just like us? Does the fact that the brain waves of the people in the study were so close to the same mean that they see things the same way, and think the same way in real life? Does that mean if you're friends with someone, whoever has the strongest personality is going to end up making the other person just like them?

We don't know! The results of scientific research are often even more questions. The only thing we can say for sure is that a friend who really "gets" us is even more amazing than we knew.

Works Cited

Parkinson, Carolyn, et al. "Similar Neural Responses Predict Friendship." *Nature Communications*, vol. 9, 2018, article 332, https://doi.org/10.1038/s41467-017-02722-7.

21

Gratitude

The desks in Ms. Johnston's room were pushed into one giant rectangle. After stopping to take off her sweatshirt layer and refill her water bottle—why was it always like a sauna in the eighth-grade wing?— Rylee was almost late to advisory. She barely took in the day's instructions on the whiteboard in the rush to her seat.

> *Joyeux Action de grâce (Canadian Thanksgiving)!*
> *Thanksgiving in Canada is the second Monday*
> *in October—a whole month and a half before*
> *American Thanksgiving—and is a low-key*
> *holiday that celebrates gratitude for the harvest*

and kicks off the winter holiday season. Question of the Day: What is a gift that you didn't want when you got it, that you've since decided was just what you needed? Think about your answer and be ready to talk thoughtfully about thankfulness today (say THAT three times fast). Welcome to advisory!

"Ni hao," Leo said as Rylee's backpack thudded onto her desk. In his black-and-teal hockey jersey, his rust-red hair seemed especially bright.

"Really, Leo?" Rylee shook her head, twisting her braids up off her neck. "Would it kill you to say 'hello' in the language of the day? What language was that, anyway?"

"Mandarin." Leo specified the Chinese dialect with his usual smug grin. "Why are you so late? Where's Dee?"

"I'm not late," Rylee said, frowning and looking toward the door. "DeNia missed homeroom, but I just saw her in the hallway. She'll be here, probably."

"Thank you for showing up to advisory!" Mr. Gil said, just as DeNia hurried in and silently handed Ms. Johnston a bright pink late pass. DeNia looked . . . weird.

"Hey. You okay?" Leo whispered as DeNia dropped into her usual seat on his other side.

"Yep," DeNia answered, but she seemed distracted. She leaned forward and waved at Rylee, then patted her pockets and pulled out a pen. She proceeded to twirl the pen between her first two fingers and her thumb as she stared at the Question of the Day, a slight frown rumpling her eyebrows.

Rylee studied DeNia closely. She could see why Leo had asked. Something was definitely . . . off with their friend. It wasn't her appearance. DeNia wore purple corduroy overalls and a white shirt. A white bandana made an adorable headband around her short Afro. She'd smiled when she came in, just like she always did. Maybe she'd had a test? Sometimes Rylee felt off after a test, and she probably looked a little weird, too.

Mr. Gil, who was wearing a knitted sweater with a giant yellow smiley on it, was halfway through discussing the worst gift he'd ever gotten—which was actually kind of a funny story about his sweater, if Rylee had been paying more attention—when it hit her what was different. DeNia's walk into the classroom had been fast, and she'd swung into her seat with a minimum of fuss, unhampered by any huge backpacks in which she could have hidden a body. The backpack at her feet today was a trim, mint-green bag with a potted-cactus print on its front and sides. Rylee had no idea how she could have missed the change.

"What happened to your backpack?" Rylee whispered, leaning forward past Leo.

DeNia raised an eyebrow, nudging the cactus bag by her foot. "Right here," she mouthed.

"No, your *backpack*. The real one," Rylee whispered.

"Excuse me, people, I am *trying* to get an education," Leo interrupted in a haughty whisper much louder than either of theirs.

Both Rylee and DeNia ignored him, though Ms. Johnston cleared her throat.

DeNia scribbled a note on the edge of Leo's desk, which Rylee couldn't read.

With a heavy sigh, Leo conveyed the message. "She said, 'This *is* my real backpack,' and she'll tell you later."

Ms. Johnston cleared her throat again, this time coming to stand behind them.

Rylee decided it was probably best to save her other questions for later.

She was grateful that their advisory exercise that day didn't require everyone saying what gift they hadn't wanted. Mr. Gil had called on a few people who volunteered, and then the whole group created a gratitude list. Ms. Johnston recorded the words onto the whiteboard and volunteers copied them with metallic-gold pen onto construction paper leaves to be included on a school-wide gratitude tree. During the breakout time, Mr. Gil gave them a choice between working on thank-you letters for the givers of the unwanted gifts or putting in more time with their self-portraits.

Though DeNia immediately set to work on a thank-you letter, using a pair of blue and black markers to design a DNA-strand stationery, Rylee couldn't imagine thanking people for things she hadn't wanted in the first place. What if that just encouraged them to give her more unwanted things? She settled down with her tacky glue and her plastic bin of paper strips.

The paper quilling self-portrait was taking *forever*. There were nine weeks left of the semester, and with a week off for November Thanksgiving, and a few teacher conference days sprinkled throughout the calendar, time for finishing was running out. As a shortcut, Rylee had just crafted a silhouette of a face out of brown construction paper, and had used braided yarn for the hair, but the brain space inside the head was still mostly empty.

At first, she'd decided to try and make it accurate,

like a real brain with tightly curled pink coils, but she'd quickly gotten bored with so much pink. She'd tried to shift the colors from pink to red, but Leo had teased that the new color scheme made her brain look like a giant valentine. In the end, she decided to add new colors and to fill the brain area with coils and arrowheads and scroll-shaped quills that would create unique patterns instead. Now the whole thing was prettier, if a little disorganized, but it did look like it was supposed to—like Rylee Swanson had a whole lot on her mind.

DeNia returned from getting more construction paper for a thank-you card and leaned against Rylee's desk. "So, I was at my class," she began.

"Dance?" Rylee still couldn't imagine DeNia running between school and extra classes three days a week while still focusing so much on grades.

"Right." DeNia kept her voice low. "Class was ending on Wednesday, and my mom came in early, so since she always freaks out if she has to wait for me, I was trying to hurry up and get ready to go, and then I tripped over my bag and just about fell on my head."

Rylee winced. DeNia's backpack was so big, that had to happen at least once a month. "Ouch. Are you okay?"

DeNia's shrugged. "Yeah, I'm a little bruised on my elbow, but I'm fine. But once she figured out I wasn't really hurt, my mom kind of yelled at me about me leaving my bag where people could trip over it. When I got to her house, I starting thinking about how sick I was of carrying it. So, yesterday, I was in Mr. Gil's classroom, and he showed me these old cabinets the school used to use for the science lab. They're these old metal lockers with little keys, and he has a couple in the corner of the lab that he's going to get rid of, but I asked him if he could let me keep my big backpack in one of them until they're gone."

"So, Mr. Gill is letting you move some of your stuff into the science lab?" Rylee grinned. "Why doesn't this surprise me, science genius?"

"Whatever." DeNia rolled her eyes. "It's just somewhere to lock up my big bag. On the days I switch houses, I can put the stuff I need for class in a small bag, and I still have everything with me, just in case, but I don't have to carry everything all day."

"That's really smart," Rylee said. "And that cactus bag is adorable—much better than that gray thing."

"Right?" DeNia grinned. "Even though it's only until Mr. Gil gets rid of those lockers, my shoulders are *here* for this tiny-backpack situation. I hope he takes all year cleaning out his messy lab."

It was almost the end of the period when the classroom door opened in a welcome swirl of cooler air. Rylee blinked, then stiffened as Nevaeh Green strolled in, holding up a bubblegum-pink hall pass—they were using paper still, since the electronic passes were offline because of some hacker—and a pair of flat brown boxes, which she placed on Ms. Johnston's desk. Ms. Johnston gave Nevaeh a thumbs-up from the front corner of the room.

Nevaeh beamed before her eyes caught Rylee's. Her smile faded, until her gaze moved to the next seat. Then the smile turned back on, as if someone had flipped a light switch.

"*Heeey*, Leo," Neveah whispered loudly, wiggling her fingers.

Rylee and DeNia exchanged a look. Both girls looked down again, Rylee so she wouldn't smirk at Leo's monotone "Hey," and DeNia—well, Rylee wasn't sure why DeNia had looked down, except she looked like she'd swallowed something unpleasant.

"Since when are you friends with her?" DeNia said,

as Nevaeh drifted over to whisper something to Aaliyah before giggling her way back into the hall.

"She's in homeroom," Leo said shortly, holding out his poster board at arm's length. For his self-portrait, Leo was drawing sixteen smaller pictures in the cubist style of Pablo Picasso. "Do you think I should add another nose to this?"

"No, you already have two on that face already," DeNia said, frowning. "Aren't these supposed to be mood self-portraits? Why do you need another nose?"

"Sometimes you're in the mood to have more noses." Leo shrugged.

"Sometimes you're in the mood to get on my last nerve," DeNia muttered.

"That's not a 'sometimes,' that's an '*always*.'" Leo grinned.

"I wonder what she put on Ms. Johnston's desk," Rylee interrupted as DeNia's eyes narrowed dangerously. "Maybe we're getting something Canadian."

Leo shrugged, sketching a third nose and another eyebrow on his portrait. "Bacon? I could deal with that."

"Leo, be *serious*," Rylee groaned, trying not to laugh. "I meant Canadian like, um . . . Canadian pennies? Or, I don't know, something thankful."

"Pennies? When we could have bacon? Rylee, Rylee." Leo was shaking his head sorrowfully, getting ready to launch into one of his usual nonsensical rants, but Rylee wasn't listening, because Aaliyah Washington was suddenly crossing the center of the room, heading directly toward her.

Oh *no*.

Even though the buzz of voices in the classroom continued as people worked on their projects, Rylee could only hear the sound of her panicked breathing, and her heart beating hard. The one thing she had dreaded for *months* was happening, right here, right now, in front of everyone. Aaliyah was going to say . . . something. Rylee wished Ms. Johnston would suddenly turn up and clear her throat again.

"Hey, Ry," Aaliyah said, tilting her head and crinkling her nose a tiny bit as she smiled. "I just had the best idea for my project. Can I have a couple of strips of paper?"

What?

Confused, Rylee silently pushed over some of her paper-shredder pile.

"Cool, thanks," Aaliyah chirped. "I only need a few."

The whole group fell silent as Aaliyah picked and chose paper strips of near the same length. She took her time, holding the pieces up to each other, concentrating. Finally, she had ten or twelve strips, and looked down at Rylee with a wide smile.

"Thanks," she said brightly, and went back to her desk.

Rylee exchanged a bewildered look with DeNia. "What just happened?" she asked nobody in particular, pulling her plastic bin of paper strips toward her again. Everything felt weird, and she had somehow gotten tacky glue on the edge of the desk. She rubbed at the spot, looking across the room. Aaliyah was working nonchalantly on her project again.

DeNia shook her head, muttered something Rylee couldn't hear and, scowling, focused on her gratitude letter.

Leo looked from Rylee to DeNia. "Ooh. Do we not like her, either?" he asked.

"Uh," Rylee began.

"*No*," DeNia said firmly, inking another black line for her DNA strand. "We do not. We're magnets, and she's the north pole."

Leo blinked in confusion. "So, she's . . . cold?" he asked tentatively.

DeNia dropped her marker and stared, horrified. "Not *the* North Pole, *a* north pole. I said we're *magnets*.

Magnets have north poles, Leo. The poles *repel* each other!" DeNia dropped her face into her hands. "Oh, my *gosh*, I cannot believe we are friends sometimes!"

"You didn't say *we* were another north pole! You just said we didn't like her," Leo protested. "What else was I supposed to think, science genius?"

Rylee tried to suppress her laughter. DeNia was completely exasperated, and she and Leo were going to argue about this the rest of the period, which was normal for them. Normal was . . . good. Rylee was shocked by how she, too, felt almost normal. Her heart wasn't rocketing around in her chest anymore, and she seriously wasn't worrying about what Aaliyah had done, or why. It was a weird moment, sure, but . . . that was it.

Rylee glanced over at her bickering friends with amused affection. DeNia could be intense about grades, and full of weird thoughts, but she had Rylee's back. Leo was a complete goof, but he was always nice, and never teased in a mean way. Rylee didn't have to waste time wondering if her friends liked her, these days, and she was grateful for DeNia's sharp mind and Leo's ability to make her laugh, even when she was annoyed.

"Huh," Rylee said in sudden realization. DeNia had

been a gift she hadn't wanted. While Leo was fast becoming a friend, his gift of humor one that Rylee hadn't known she would need, DeNia had been there from the first, pulling Rylee out of her comfort zone, forcing her to see things a different way.

Rylee also remembered Devon and Cam leaning over the Mouse Guard book with her, laughing. Without even noticing she had begun the journey, Rylee realized that she had finished it. She was on the other side of that giant canyon she'd felt open inside her on the first day of school, when she was certain she'd never have another friend. Somehow, she'd found out how to build a bridge, and she'd made it over.

Though she would never thank them for it, maybe the Spite Sisters had done her more of a favor than they would ever know.

The *Segrest Sentinel* Reports

Friendship Sidebar: Be Alone, Not Lonely
by Rylee Swanson

***

Throughout the semester, eighth graders DeNia Alonso and Rylee Swanson will be reporting on different aspects of friendship and how it affects those of us in junior high.

***

New classmates, teachers, and a huge new campus made starting middle school super intimidating. I worried a lot about not knowing anyone and never finding friends. When my mom saw I was freaking out, she said I would be okay if I planned on being by myself sometimes. That sounded . . . weird, but she was right. If you're not talking to your friends, have a different lunch period from anyone you know, or are new to Segrest School, this article is for you.

Planning to be by yourself is easy. If you have a plan, you can pack a special treat or a fun activity like a manga comic with your lunch. You can bring an adventure book, a romance, or a DIY book to learn origami. If you are an eighth grader with phone privileges during lunch, you can watch a DIY video and learn something cool like needle felting or calligraphy. Planning ahead can help you feel less like a self-conscious dork and more like yourself, just having some you-time.

It doesn't matter if you're a new sixth grader or an eighth grader who has been here a while; being alone sometimes happens to everyone! Remembering that can help you feel less lonely, and less like something is wrong with you. If you feel super uncomfortable:

During homeroom, get a library pass to be in the library during lunch. (Remember: no food or drink in there. Don't make Mr. Blaine kick you out.)

Join a club. Many clubs meet in the library during lunch. The Gamers Group is always looking for new players.

Try sitting in an empty chair at a table

with a group. When you sit down, smile and say "hi." You might make new friends. If they're not friendly, next time move on, and try another group.

Try sitting at a table filled with lots of people sitting by themselves. It's sometimes more comfortable to be alone with other alone people.

Maybe find a spot outside to listen to music, soak up the sun, or take a quick nap (pro tip: SET AN ALARM!!!).

There are so many things to do other than feel sad because you're not with friends. If you're by yourself, OWN IT. Be friendly to yourself. You are good company, and you're worth spending time with.

22

What Happened After

The three-toned bell marked the close of another day at Segrest School, and an avalanche of bodies burst from classrooms and filled the hallway, sweeping a tumble of eager students toward the exits. A cloudburst drenching the world beyond the glass doors, however, slowed the process of the exodus. The courageous were screaming and bolting toward their rides or the shelter of the bus kiosk, while the rest lingered under the sheltered portico to dig for umbrellas or lament the puddles that awaited them.

"It's so weird not to have to *dig* in this thing," DeNia was saying, hoisting her backpack and twirling the compact umbrella she'd just taken from its zippered interior.

"I don't need everything in my big bag until after school on Monday. Dad's picking me up today, and we're just going to go to the hardware store. We're building a bookshelf for my room and repainting the dresser."

"That sounds fun. I should do something cool with my room this weekend." Rylee dodged an elbow and pulled up her raincoat hood. Ugh, she wasn't looking forward to going out in the weather at *all*. "I'm taking the bus today. Are you going to wait for your dad outside?"

"No," DeNia said, standing on tiptoe to look over the crowd. "I'll walk you to the bus stop, though, if you want."

"That's okay—" Rylee began, but saw Devon standing in the middle of the crowd of students closest to the door. She waved.

"Have you seen Cameron?" Devon called. "We were planning to meet out front and walk to my house, and I think I'm the only one with an umbrella."

"Sorry," Rylee said, glaring at the sky. She pushed through the packed hallway to get closer. "Did you text? There are so many people in here, they might be waiting outside."

"I did," Devon said. "My phone is dying, though. Can I borrow yours?"

Rylee dug into her jeans pocket, turning as DeNia waded through the crowd to her side. "Devon, you know DeNia, right? She's the one I've been working with on the paper. You should let her tell you what you did for science fair in sixth grade."

DeNia gave an embarrassed laugh and stepped closer, shifting a little to stand nearer to the open double doors as another trickle of students splashed toward their rides.

"No, you shouldn't," she said. "Hey, Devon. I think we were seatmates first semester in Forum last year."

"Oh, right." Devon smiled. "I missed you second semester. You were the only person in our whole row who shared their snacks."

DeNia chuckled. "Well." She turned and peered through the doorway as a truck pulled forward in the pickup line. "Oh—there's my dad. I'll see you guys."

"I wish someone was picking me up," sighed Devon as DeNia waved a goodbye and plunged into the deluge. She handed back Rylee's phone. "I sent a text, but if Cam's not here in five minutes, I'm going to go. It's supposed to start raining harder by four."

"Ugh. I might just go, too," Rylee said, pulling up her turtleneck and wishing she had a warmer hat than just the plastic hood of her raincoat. "I can't see waiting for the bus in this."

Someone squealed as a gust of wind sent umbrellas flying. For the moment, it seemed like the rain had diminished, but the rising wind was whipping the puddles, spraying water and mist into everyone's faces.

Rylee scrunched up her face. "Okay, seriously, I think I'm going to make a run for it," she decided. "Do you want to come over later, Dev? If you and Cameron don't have any special gaming stuff to do, I mean?" When there wasn't an immediate answer, Rylee turned. "Dev?"

Rylee did a double take as Aaliyah Washington stepped around Devon, approaching Rylee with a smile. "Hey! You're not seriously walking home in this, are you? Come wait with us. My mom's coming, and she can drop you off."

Rylee froze, feeling a mixture of surprise and . . . something like nervousness. Aaliyah was doing it again, talking like she had in advisory, as if nothing had ever gone on between them. Rylee blinked, knowing she probably looked like a deer stunned by headlights.

"Isn't this weather wild? I can't believe it's not even Christmas yet, and it's already so cold. It's ridiculous!" Aaliyah continued, twirling the large, sky-blue golf umbrella she was carrying. "Did you see what I was making in advisory? My self-portrait project is turning out so cute. Your quilling project is amazing, though. I can't believe you did all that work. Those little pieces of paper are so tiny, and there's, like, a million of them."

Her manners kicked in and Rylee opened her mouth to mumble a thank-you, then stopped herself, chewing her lip. Wait, what was she doing? Aaliyah was not a friend, and this wasn't a normal, friendly conversation. Aaliyah was chatting in an open, friendly way, pretending like nothing had happened between them, but Rylee . . . couldn't. She wouldn't.

"And I can't believe how talented Leo is," Aaliyah was saying, leaning in, her expression warm with amused disbelief. "I can't believe how much he talks to you, either. Nevaeh sits by him in homeroom, and she says he's so shy, she can't even get him to say anything. She could not believe you were sitting with him and he was saying things."

Oh. Rylee exhaled in relief as it all clicked into place. Aaliyah's sudden attack of friendly behavior and beginning conversations. "It's Leo?" she blurted. "All of this is about *Leo Riesen?*"

"What?" Aaliyah said, frowning at the interruption. "What are you talking about? I don't know what 'it' means. I was just saying Leo—"

"He talks all the time," interrupted Rylee. "Just so you know. Leo's not even a little bit shy," she blurted.

"Well, I've never talked to him, so I wouldn't know," Aaliyah sputtered.

"I'm just saying." Rylee stifled a laugh, imagining DeNia's horrified face when she told her about this. Then she winced, imagining *Leo's*. Poor Leo. "If Leo doesn't talk to Nevaeh, it's definitely not because he's shy. So . . . yeah."

Done talking, Rylee stepped around Aaliyah, knowing her audience had to be close by. Sure enough, Cherise and Nevaeh were huddled beneath an umbrella a few feet away from the door. Rosario stood tall under her rain poncho, looking out at the parking lot with the same perpetually bored expression that was usually on her face. And at the very edge of the sidewalk, half-turned toward the street, Devon was standing uncertainly with her umbrella raised, looking like she wasn't sure that she should wait.

Oh. Devon. She'd left her friend waiting for her once before, hadn't she?

As the wind caught her hood, a spatter of water sluiced down Rylee's cheek, sparking a memory of crawling goose bumps and shame. But this water was clean and fresh, free of chlorine and bad memories, and today, the distance between herself and a friend could be crossed with only a few steps.

"I'm coming with you, Devon." Rylee skirted around the last clump of students waiting out the rain and jogged forward. "Hey, look—is that Cam across the street at the bus stop?"

A bus pulling away from the stop on the opposite side of the road revealed a lone, soggy figure in a blue sweatshirt waving an arm.

"Oh, yay! Finally!" Devon said, relieved, and raised her umbrella.

Rylee grasped the edge of her hood and dodged a puddle as they paused at the crosswalk.

From behind, they heard an indignant shout. "Rylee! What are you doing—! *Hey!* We're waiting for my mother!" Aaliyah sounded irritated and confused.

"No, thanks. I'm going with my friends," Rylee yelled back, and ran to where her real ones were waiting.